The Shadow and the Song

by

Michael Gilderdale

Grosvenor House
Publishing Limited

Michael Gilderdale is hereby identified as author of this
work in accordance with Section 77 of the Copyright, Designs
and Patents Act 1988

The book cover picture is copyright to Michael Gilderdale

This book is published by
Grosvenor House Publishing Ltd
28-30 High Street, Guildford, Surrey, GU1 3HY.
www.grosvenorhousepublishing.co.uk

A CIP record for this book
is available from the British Library

ISBN 978-1-907211-49-2

Also by the author

✳✳✳

How to be Happy while you are Here
Last Bus to Primrose Hill
My most chosen Friends
A Place by the Sea
A Plain Man's Guide to the Asylum

To La Muchacha dorada
For all your unstinting help.

And muchos gracias
Holly and Manolo Frias
for information, encouragement
and the translation of the Sonnet in tribute
to Manuel de Falla, offering him flowers.

Cover image by Fernando Fernandez
shows Capileira, Alpujarras,
Sierra Nevada, Granada province, Andalusia, Spain.

'Through the laurel's branches
I saw two dark doves.
One was the sun
The other the moon.
Little neighbours, I called,
Where is my tomb?
In my tail, said the sun,
In my throat, said the moon.'

(Trans. Christopher Maurer, Collected Poems).

Part One

A Most Unusual Boy

It was in the time before the rivers of the eight Provinces were stained with the blood of innocents and murderers alike. The two men sat at an open fire on the flat lands, the *Vega* below Granada. They sprawled by the smouldering embers in a silence broken only by the bell-like chime of the harnesses on their two horses dipping and raising their heads impatiently. The dying sun sucked little warmth from the soil. Carlos, a young rifleman bound, he hoped, for the Guardia Civil, chucked the but end of his cigar into the fire and spat.

"Well, you son of a whore, so you think the *campesinos* (peasants) are making big problems for us, eh?"

Perez, a *Funcionario del Estado* — a young union official — simpler than his title suggested, said "Carlos, you speak crap. Are you blind? Where is the harvest. We have no rain and now there are many families starving. It is certain. There must be trouble."

Carlos grinned. "A good year then to kill wolves in Cordoba."

Perez did not understand what he meant. Carlos added "Let them eat shit!"

It was also a time in the early 20th century when the Americans had left Cuba to Gomez, and when many died in an attempted revolution in Catalunia. By contrast it was also the time when a young schoolmaster in Granada called Luis Castejou was setting out pen and paper, even before the sun was up, to make a start on a Journal he wished to write. His words, he hoped, would salute the fame of his ancient and beloved Granada.

※※※

1

What Luis wrote began as follows: The child is father to the man. You could say that is stupid. An impossibility. Except, out of the mouths of babes and sucklings. Are not those words found in The Good Book, Matthew 21? I never understood their meaning, but the words always remained in my head. You can believe them if your brain is losing its connections like the poor fellow who was so troubled by them he jumped into the waters of the Guadalquivir. I would not do it. I love my life. I love my Granada. It is, and always will be, my home.

As a teacher it is my duty to develop and encourage the minds of my pupils, to lead them in the right path, to teach them to observe, to listen, to obey and in the end to help them decide which turning they should take when, in their wisdom, they have grown young again. It is called education and is now happening more in my country of different languages, customs and climates. It is a curious thing to do maybe, but the Good Lord has decided I must write. There is no escape. No true born Spaniard can escape their destiny, and I am a Granadino from my head to my toes. It is true. I was born here in Granada, the best place in the world which, after so many years of weeping, the Good Lord is going to make beautiful again. And that I believe to be a miracle which can happen.

My school, I admit, is not of the best. The *conventos* are often considered to be better because the Church has the money. Also I am not the head of my *escuela* of the Sacred Heart because I did not have money to finish my studies at the University. My headmaster is the Padre Suarez who is sometimes difficult to understand. A most religious man, but very shy. The building of my school needs attention but will not get it yet. We are not in the centre of the city but near to the Albaicin, painted with the same brush as the Moorish tribes and now the *gitane, the* gypsies who live there. No matter. I am proud of my school. No other is like it. There are those in Granada who say it is too *moderno* but the good Padre and I take little notice because the council allows it. We have an architectural staircase. You enter, climb stairs to a small hall. There are more stairs to the left to where the Padre takes Mass and teaches the Holy Bible. The stairs to the right are to a large room where I teach the subjects my boys must have including numbers, writing, reading, nature, geography, and now some history. The number of boys I teach is not many, but there is one who is not like the others. He sits at the end of the room by the window and sometimes I think maybe he is asleep. But his eyes do not close and he is looking as if to see a far away place, another land. But that cannot be. Is he dreaming all the time of his home? After all it is not so far distant. It is a good home. I have known it since the boy — he is called Federico — was four years old. The family live close to the village of Fuente Vaqueros, twelve miles away and on the *vega*. The name is Garcia Rodriguez but from the Father's marriage it is known as Lorca, from the mother, Dona Vicenta Lorca Romero. And it is a good home, a quite big *granja*. And rich. It has *trigo e callo* (wheat and maize), also *aceitunos* (olives) and many horses. Also mules. No other farm has so much.

I say that Federico Lorca is a different boy and this may be because of his left leg. He has been limping since he was four years of age. His mother said it was from birth. He cannot play The Tail of The Cat with the other boys. He is sometimes sad and then, as if waking from sleep, he becomes very noisy and happy. I do not understand him but he is quite clever, good with numbers and he likes to sing and give a performance with imitations. Soon after he came to my school I learned how he spent his time at home. He liked to go with the cattle men on the Vega and also in the garden he would invent little plays. He goes to church with his mother and once dressed up as a priest and conducted Mass with a small statue of the virgin on the garden wall. The servants of the house were commanded to attend his performance, also his aunts and cousins, for he wanted an audience. He was certainly a different kind of priest because as well as giving a song he would strum on a *guitarra*! He had also built a toy theatre with his brother Francisco and persuaded one of the servants in the house to make puppets for it. With them he devised plays and, it was said, added a name and a different voice to each character. My wife is better at understanding young children, even though we do not have one of our own. She gives attention to Federico and has come to love him as if he was her child.

Now, I should mention my wife. She would not forgive me if I seem to forget her. How could I? We are happy together. She is not a teacher now, but she was when I first met her. How we are married? It is unusual, because she is from a Portuguese family, and that is not very popular in Granada. A year after coming to my school I was directed to a new course for teachers in Cordoba. A *congresso internacional*. It was important because *estudianta* came from many places and it was for one week, intensive. On the first day I had to check my name and details at the recepcion, the welcome desk, and there I found this girl also giving her name which was Sophia Pereira. Immediately I found her beautiful, small of build with a smiling face and a crown of dark hair tied back like a horses tail. Her eyes were green as an almond shell.

I said *"Encantado!* You are from Cordoba?"

She shook her head but gave me a happy look and replied "Boa tarde!" So then I knew she was Portuguese. I was confused and all I could say was "I Luis Castejou. Granada. Pleased to meet you."

"Muito prazer!" Again a lovely smile on her lips and in her green eyes which I liked very much because they also smiled. The next time, between classes, we were in the refectory and it was like being at university again. We found the same table. And we found each other.

"You have come a long way from your home, Sophia?"

She understood quite well and replied "My family is from Barcelos near Braga. The Minho, to the north, but I am now staying in Cordoba."

I had more questions because she was very friendly. She said she was teaching in a school for young children where she could earn more money than in Portugal. She was living in the home of her cousins. I studied her closely and had strong feelings because in my view she was so beautiful, delicate and a pale skin with no lines, and slender hands. She was also *mucha cortesmente.* (very polite). Her family was from the line of Cruz Pereira, a known artist whose fathers' paintings were in several countries. But there was sadness. She said her mother and her father had died, but I was not sure it was the truth. I think more likely they had separated and gone on different paths. It was all most interesting and, as we say at home, soon we are drinking from the same cup. At least I think she liked me and said that when the conference ended we could be friends by post. I would write of my school and she could do the same from Cordoba. I was happy and in seven days we took many glasses together and, I confess, in the evening there was a kiss I did not expect!

From the beginning we were drawn together, liking the same things. I wanted always to be with her. We exchanged letters every week, and to make my journal not too long here I mention the occasion when we were to be married. It was not the best time because in the north there had been a strike with very bad riots, with killing and the burning of churches. It was also reported that in Morocco fierce tribes were attacking our soldiers. No, not a good time, with violence in some towns, but I was hot for love and Sophia agreed we would not wait for better times to prevail. Then, we are arguing. I said we should be married in Granada, but Sophia wanted Cordoba. I said it had to be family and my family was Granada but she had only cousins in Cordoba. It was a bit unkind but I had my way. I thought all was agreed. But then to my amazement she said it would not be a church but in the *campo.* The countryside.

"Please, Luis you must listen! My mother and father were married in the *campo* but first a blessing in the church. It was near Ponta da Barca beside the waters of the river Lima, very beautiful with the tall trees and an ancient bridge. There the priest came to join their hands and that is what I would like, beside the water open to the sky and where in the silence there is only birds singing. No, Luis, I am serious. That is how I also should be married."

I did not know what to say. The birds singing? It was most unexpected and I had to think very hard. It was uncomfortable for me.

5

I realised that Portuguese people are not like my people, but I could see she was determined and my heart said, and my head, that I must not lose her. The end of my confession. It was in August that we became man and wife, yes, by a river. the Guadajoz, some few miles south of Cordoba with the priest, her two cousins, and my step-mother after we had been in the church of La Magdalena. Sophia was sad that her brother and her sister who was also a teacher could not come to us from Braga. We had no money for a holiday but all together we had a celebration in the restaurante Isabel, and I was very happy because I was deeply lost in my love for Sophia, and she with me. It was several months later that she came to my home in Granada, but of course, she did not teach any more.

Now, a coincidence, but true. Dona Vicenta, the mother of the boy Lorca, sent a message that I must see her. I went down to the farm. I knew her a little and I admired her. She had been something of a teacher herself and she gave her son Federico his first lessons. Dona Vicenta was very welcoming. She called a maidservant and I was offered a plate of *jamon* with *aceitunas* and a glass of wine which, she explained was made from grapes in the small vineyard. She was very observant, as I always knew.

"I see Senor Castejou you are limping like my Federico."

"Yes, ma'am I confess it."

"You had the illness like my son?"

"No, not illness. Some years ago, when I was a boy I liked to walk in the Sierra, and when I have the time this I still do."

"She shook her head and gave a smile. "Ah boys! Boys! Always look-ing for adventure!"

"No, no! I was not brave."

"You were going to climb to Mulhacen in the snow? There, I cannot believe it! Even my husband has not climbed, it is too high, and dangerous."

"No ma'am, not on the mountain. I was on the lower slopes, collecting."

She looked at me long and hard. After a silence she said "You are a naturalist. I am surprised."

I told her that I did like flowers, and that I still collect them for the classroom, because it was part of my teaching of nature. The violet, the wild rose and the chamomile, and honeysuckle. I said how good it was to explore through the forest, the beautiful trees of alder, ash and the shade of the willow. Then I stopped saying this because I felt the wine was going to my head. Also I did not know why she had called me to see her.

Another silence and I was embarrassed. Then the good Dona Vicenta said "All this walking. And now you are limping ."

The rivers and streams I told her were full from the snows above. They were flowing fast and difficult to cross. I explained how I had slipped and broken my ankle. It had not been repaired in time and was sometimes painful.

"I am sorry to hear it. That was foolish. A teacher of my boy should be more careful. You have now learned a lesson." And she added "My Federico likes flowers, did you know?"

I replied that he took some interest in them. She was silent, then surprised me by saying "He now wishes to learn the guitarra. You will arrange it please. At home I am teaching him to play the piano. He shows some ability. I think he will be musical. My family, and the family of my husband also liked to play music."

This I knew. But, Dona Vicenta, I believed, was a religious person and I wondered why she did not make her enquiries with the Padre Suarez who, after all, was the head of my school. She replied that she had seen him, but had changed her mind.

"I have spoken with him of course, but it is too difficult. When he comes to me, which is not very often, he sits and says nothing.

Not a word unless we discuss affairs of the church. Then he whispers and I cannot find any conversation with him. I am sure he is a good man but until he has some manners I cannot have any use of him."

And that was that. She herself had no more to say, except when she held the door for me she added "I expect you have found my Federico very talkative. And he is. He will speak to flowers and trees as if they were people. Did you know he gives them names? I find this unusual. It touches my heart, but you must not notice it."

I was not altogether surprised. I was becoming used to the boy's ways, sometimes silent but more usually he would become suddenly noisy and full of laughter. I remembered to thank Dona Vicenta for the *jamon*, then took my way back up to the city thinking that talking to flowers was not so strange. Perhaps the boy was lonely, or maybe his father did not love him. That I felt was hard to believe. The Rodrigues were rich, and a good family. I am sure there was much love, because Federico in some way was more sensitive than many others of his age, even his brother and sister. I think he needed to know he was loved.

In the evenings, instead of the *paseo* I would sometimes take Sophia with me to the Mirador, a tapas near Plaza de los Lobos. Alberto Frias was famous as the oldest owner of any café from the Alhambra to Sevilla. No one ever knew his age, but we accepted that he was history. He would know, and on this particular evening I asked him. Not for his age, but for information. He would sometimes sit at the table with me and leave the serving to his son and the gypsy woman he employed. He always coughed strongly into his beard, then illuminated a new cigar, and on this evening he blew the smoke into the still air above Sophia's head.

"*Caliente!* he muttered. "*Mucho.*"

Did I not *know* it ! Even the air was burning bare arms. Before mid-day it had been 37o C.

"Tell me old chap," I began. "I have a question. You will know who is the best teacher of the guitarra here in Granada?" Alberto was looking with interest at Sophia. He blew another curl of smoke above her head and asked "It is you who will learn the guitarra?"

Sophia laughed. "No, no! I love music but I do not play"

I said "It is Federico, the Rodriguez boy. His mother asks me for him"

Alberto shook his grizzled head like an old toro avoiding the *muleta* in the corrida. He then had another fit of coughing and grunted "Not the *universidad*. It is better to speak with the *gitane.*"

Sophia said "I have heard there are many here in Granada. Also in Cordoba. They are famous with their flamenco."

Alberto was nodding his head. "You are right *muchacha*. The gypsies. They can be intelligente with excellent music, but some are also intelligente with stealing and the knife. Everyone knows, they will murder to get pesetas for their pleasure."

He put down his cigar and tapping a forefinger on the back of his hand he winked and put his hand to his nose and sniffed. Then he picked up the half of his cigar that was still burning. He grinned. "I am too old now. This is my pleasure!"

I was alarmed. "But, can you be serious my friend? A young lad from the fine home of Don Rodriguez to go to the gypsies for a lesson? I feel they would forbid it."

In a voice like a rubbing of stones in a drying river bed Alberto called out to his son, Santos. "Get that idle bum of yours over here and bring us three beers. pronto, or we die of thirst!" He turned to me. "Please, it is my *regalo* (treat) for your beautiful wife. You are a fortunate fellow!"

Three large bottles arrived on the table. I thanked Alberto warmly. We were parched. All was quiet. Just the birds circling and calling outside above the plaza. We finished our second bottles and Alberto again came to life. He said "I recommend that you tell the boy to find Francisco da Silva Camaron, or Jose Manuel Lopez. Each of them is skilled in Flamenco guitarra. He can go to the caves and there he should make enquiries."

Sophia gave me a quick elbow in my side and whispered "The boy cannot go alone, it would not be safe." I did not require to be told. I thanked Alberto again and said I would arrange to accompany Federico to the gitane. As we departed Alberto rose from his chair and shouted. "Remember, tell the boy he cannot learn in one turning of the moon. It is not like the peeling of a *cebolla!*"

I heard him cough and spit, and call again to his son.

I am not impatient by nature. If your choice is to earn a living, however modest, by teaching young children then you must cultivate a quiet patience. The *ninos* deserve every care you can give. On the next Sunday morning with the bells ringing their welcome across the newly washed streets, and with a thin air blowing from the sierra to caress my skin, I had a song in my heart. But, then it died. It is not my nature but I became anxious, and disappointed. I was waiting for the boy Lorca to turn up but he did not. He was to arrive at the school when, as arranged, I would take him to find the gypsies spoken of by Alberto.

For one hour I waited, but no boy came. Finally, quite angry, I decided he must be at his home. I would find him. I borrowed a *caballito* (pony) from my neighbour, saddled up, and rode down to the farm. The family had just moved to a small place called Asquerosa and bought more land on an estate several miles away where the main crop was sugar beet which paid good money. There I met Don Rodriguez, the boy's father who enquired of my visit. I dismounted, and tied the good *caballito* to the gate.

"Disculpe, muito gusto senor! I am seeking your son Federico, and cannot find him. Is he by chance with you? I am worried because today I am to take him for his lessons on the guitarra but he did not arrive at the school."

Senor Rodriquez is a tall and strong man and very successful. He is much admired for his business ability. I knew that he had lost his first wife, but married again and it was only a year before Federico had been born. I was somewhat in awe of him, but it was not necessary. He had a dark countenance, heavy brows but a cheerful manner. It was said, and I hoped it was true, that he had a sense of humour.

He looked down upon me and frowned. "Guitarra?" he exclaimed. "What is my boy doing with the guittara? He is quite musical, my wife teaches him pianoforte, but he has no time for lessons on the guittara. I was not aware that your school teaches music."

I explained that the lessons would not be at school. He asked where I had planned for Federico to be taught. When I told him that my intention was to take Federico to find a gipsy, a professional in flamenco at Sacromonte, his mood abruptly darkened.

"Now see here, schoolmaster, that is a foolish idea, and I will not allow it. The gitane are not to be relied on, and apart from that, while music may be a pleasing pastime it is not a career. Today, I have sent him to the new estate. He likes to be with the cattle men. When he is ready my boy will go to the university and prepare for a proper career. He must study. He has a strong intelligence. My intention is for him to become a lawyer."

I was now in some difficulty. Summoning my courage I said "With respect, sir, it is your wife who asked that he be taught guittara. I have said I would arrange it."

"But you will not. You may think I am unreasonable, but that is not so. My family, also my wife's family are musical. They have been quite famous for singing. But music is no career for my boy. You waste your time, and mine. I will speak with my wife, and there's an end to it. I will explain, and you need have no worry. Now, I must ask you to leave, I am delayed and have much work."

I was dismayed. Then, as he was about to turn away he said "Please remember what I am telling you. I wish you well. I think you have a good school, but leave the music. At my boy's age History, Language, Latin is the correct discipline is it not?" Then he added with an unexpected gentleness in his voice. "See here, I'd give that *caballito* of yours some good corn, or his poor legs will not carry him, or you, from here to the river."

I admired the man, but I was disappointed. Now there was a problem on my plate and I was not hungry for it. The farmer was a good man. Yes, yes, I thought to myself I do not mind if he has many horses and a fine *granja*, but he was being unreasonable. Mother Mary, Mother of Grace, forgive me but I was in a mood to curse him! I turned away and leading my *caballito* I trod slowly back to the city with no cheerfulness. That family must decide about the boy, but I still felt I should find a way to do as Dona Vicenta required of me. I had little sleep that night, but I spoke with Sophia and found her agreement. On the following day as the school bell rang for the end of classes I told Federico he was to come with me to Sacromonte and there we would speak with the gitane. It was becoming dark but even at some distance you could see the fires they always light, not for warmth but for the big pot into which someone said they would throw anything and everything except their horses or the grandmother.

I took Federico's hand. He was very excited for he had been forbidden to see the caves before. As we approached we were met by a plump lady, poorly clad in a torn dress of red and a with black shawl at her shoulders. She scowled and her pocked face resembled a dark, rough geographia, a crumpled *terrano* that had seen many storms. She was suspicious and her voice was cracked and coarse.

"What do you want, gringo, with that child?" She stared hard at Federico, then grinned. "I could eat him, he is *durazno* (pretty as a peach). Why are you here?" She called over her shoulder "Juan ! Here is a caballero with *joven* come to visit!"

A tall, slim fellow wearing a white blouse tucked into his leggings stepped forward and trod carefully round the fire. He was perhaps twenty years of age and had a noble face. His eyes sought mine. "Mucho gusta!"

I replied that I, too, was pleased to meet with him, and wished to explain our visit.

"My name is Castejou. I am from the school of the Sacred Heart and here is a pupil from my class. His name is Federico Lorca of the Rodriguez family. He wishes to learn to play guitarra and it is said you can teach him. Is this possible?"

The old witch immediately answered. "Juan will not, he does not play. He is a dancer, very good. Electrica! But I have two sons and they are maravilla!" She rolled her eyes. "Maravilla from Sevilla! They are the best!"

She offered another awful grin and was pleased with her rhyme. Then she looked questioningly at Juan. He put his hand to his face, and after a pause he said "It is unusual, the boy is very young. I think I have seen him sometime among the cattle men at the Genil. Please remain. I will ask." He turned and went into the house which was made in the side of the cliff.

We waited, and the impression I received was that maybe he thought it impossible for a lad to play, for how could one so young learn flamenco guitarra.

We waited even longer, but when he returned Juan said we should go with him into his house. It was a little dark but from the fire our shadows moved on the plain walls. I was worried that Federico was tongue-tied. He had spoken not one word and I thought perhaps he was afraid. I was wrong. He pulled his hand from mine and raising both arms he looked about him wide-eyed and called out *"hermoso! E Lindo!"* ("Lovely!").

It was a relief, and it was then that Juan called two men who came from a back room The old witch said, proudly, "Here are my sons, Francisco and Jose Manuel Lopez! They are often playing in Sevilla!"

Juan introduced the men. They nodded but said nothing. Juan said "They are from different families."

It would certainly seem to be so because while Franciso was tall, with a head of hair beginning to turn grey, Jose was small, dark and with a fat belly. They did not appear to be friendly and I doubted they could be brothers. It was indicated that we should sit on the only two chairs visible and wait. The two men and Juan disappeared into the back room and we heard voices loudly raised. They then returned. Juan began. "We must discuss. It is a question of the money." Turning to me he asked "How much will be paid?"

This I had not expected. But of course, as a teacher I should have been prepared. All lessons must be paid for. Juan repeated the question. "Well, my friend what do you say? How much?"

The one called Francisco observed "We are glad to see you." And looking to Federico he added "He is a pretty boy!" I thanked him, but trying to consider payment I found I had no sensible suggestion to make. I simply did not know. The Rodriquez were rich enough, and the gypsies, even those thought to be fair - minded, always needed money, sometimes begging on the street. I said it was difficult for me to speak for the Rodriguez but if they said a sum I would find out if the family would agree it.

Then Francisco spoke again. "I think for six lessons first it should be one hundred pesetas. We can then decide if the boy should continue."

14

Jose Manuel turned on him and growled "I have said that is not enough, the price is wrong it should be three hundred!"

"Of course!" croaked the plump lady. "It is skill you pay for, three hundred is the cost!"

Francisco held his ground. "No, no! You are wrong! We are not criminal. You want to skin our friend like a rabbit?"

Voices were again raised, and it was difficult to understand because they spoke in their gypsy language and I knew little of it. Jose cried "It is your weakness! You do not think of winter or what we shall have! May your balls freeze in hell! I skin YOU like a rabbit! He shouted still louder. "I say 300 or nothing!" He whipped a knife from his pocket, flicked it open and advanced on Francisco who then seized a stick from the fire and the two of them circled crouching and ready to strike. Alarmed, I grabbed Federico and pushed him behind me. This was a bad situation and could be dangerous. The two 'brothers' had, in the blinking of an eye, become animals and I did not like their intention. Without more thought, but with some risk, I too raised my voice. "No! Halt!" And I attempted to jump between them. It was a foolish thing to do for the raised knife hit my hand and blood flowed even as Juan struggled to separate the brothers.

I write no more of this of which I stand ashamed. I was foolish, but the cut was not deep. I was more alarmed about the boy. It was a surprise that he did not seem to be afraid. He was simply standing there and watching as if it was an entertainment. The old crone shook her head. "You must go. Come back another time and we will agree something." She waved us away. "Always the same! The love of brothers. They will kill each other."

In the end, of course, they did not. All was settled. Dona Vicenta sent the message "I will pay the gitane 300 pesetas but not more."

I did as she instructed, and then I chose not to return again to the *cuvea*s, for I had no heart to become further involved with family

15

disagreement. As it happened it was not necessary. I learned that the boy had found a way round his father's wishes. It seemed that Federico was very sure of himself. He went alone to the gitane. He liked them and said they were good to him.

Two years passed and apart from school I did not see very much of Federico. I visited Dona Vicenta from time to time to report on her son's progress in class. She told me he was now playing guitarra with some skill and was equally talented with his piano lessons.

❋❋❋

After several years all was change. The Rodriguez family moved to a fine house in Granada called La Huerta de San Vicente and after good progress at school Federico was enrolled at the university to learn Law which I suspect he did not enjoy. He much preferred other subjects, mainly the plays of Shakespeare and Ibsen in translation, Checkov and early Spanish poets. His skill with the guitarra continued, and he was also spending time for piano lessons at the conservatory. He seemed to be very happy and loved to sing and to recite. It was Sophia who first told me about his poems. We were taking our evening stroll and called at the Mirador as was our custom. Often a friend came to our table. One such person was Sanchez Carvajal. He sometimes escaped from his office to join us for a drink. At that time he was General Manager of El Mensajero a quite popular newspaper in competition with our local rag, the Heraldo de Granada.

"I was impressed," Sophia was saying. "We should raise a glass to the boy Federico. My friend Teresa said he came several times to her mother's house where he played the piano and sang some beautiful songs. I can believe it. Only yesterday I was passing by the Plaza, and he was playing guitarra, and singing. There was a crowd standing there and they liked him very much."

"I am not surprised," Sanchez replied. "I also have seen him. I am told he composes his own songs, and poetry as well. He is a fine looking lad, a champion for our city and a good influence. As a musician I think he could be a success!".

Well, I was pleased. He was my pupil. Had I not been the first to encourage his interest with music when we visited the gitane? "I cannot imagine," I added, "what his family may think. His mother is musical but his father is interested only in the farm, and the profit he can make. I wonder he has not prevented Federico. He could destroy his talent."

Sanchez kindly ordered another drink for us, and said "If the boy was taught by those gitane in the Sacromento he will never forget his music."

The conversation then turned to more important observations. Sanchez surprised me by saying he was not superstitious, but when the wind blew across the sierra very strongly from Africa and made the bells of St Nicholas ring and the birds fly up like a black cloud he had a *presentimiento* (a premonition). "I suspect more trouble is coming our way. Mark my words. We already have the reports."

Sophia gave him a questioning look. "You mean the rumours from Catalunia? I have heard them too, but I cannot believe them."

"They are more than rumours, young woman," said Sanchez. "Unhappily it is the truth."

At the moment Alberto appeared from his doorway, advanced to our table and growled "Hola, schoolteacher! Como esta?"

I said that I was well.

"I also!" So saying he took the empty chair and joined our little party.

Sanchez teased him. "Hey you old slug, are you still crawling around? I was speaking of the bells of St. Nicholas!"

Alberto interrupted "Not a problem. Alberto is here with his forceful café, you need have no fear!"

Sanchez was serious. He said the situation in the North was becoming worse. "The reports can be read in my paper. Also in the Heraldo. They are mad up there, behaving like the Russians. Bolchies!"

I knew what he meant. Two trade unions were making trouble in Catalunia. There had been strikes and now violence was spreading from Barcelona to Bilbao. There was also continuing war in the colonies, in Cuba and Morocco.

"In my view the fault is with Maura," said Sanchez. "He demanded call-up for the Army and those anarchists did not like it. Took to violence, even burning down churches! People died! I tell you, if Canalejas takes over, that is the only hope." He paused and allowed the suspicion of a wicked smile to cross his face. "After all, is not Canalejas a journalist? We need a Liberal, if the King allows it."

"He will." rumbled Alberto. "Alfonso can make no difference, he can do nothing."

I said I felt glad that we did not have that kind of trouble in Granada, for after all it was generally agreed that we have little violence here. We are a city by tradition very beautiful, rich in history, poetry and song.

"Do not be so sure that we can always avoid trouble," replied Sanchez. "We have political division like other places. And after all, here in the south, in Cordoba, in Sevilla or even Cadiz there is nothing to prevent a butcher, a shoemaker or an ambitious *genoma* (gnome) in the Union General de Trabajadires getting to his feet, gathering comrades around him, and putting up a flag for the anarchists!"

Sophia, who had been listening intently, exclaimed "May God forbid! Then there would be no more singing from our Federico!"

"Nah, nah!"Alberto interrupted, illuminating a comfortable cigar. "If he is with the gitanos he will have no trouble."

I thought that was true. Here, where flamenco is now adding to our entertainments, we know we can be happy just like those princes of fortune who made their great palace all those years ago with its gardens and fountains. Perhaps we should send our politicians to the Generalife to sit together and reflect. And then I reminded myself it might not be so simple. While here in Granada we have dancing and music, and cafes, a university and many fine buildings, outside the city there are only peasants with no education. Most of them cannot read or write. Life is not fair to them. They are very poor and unable to help themselves.

✳✳✳

On the evening of my birthday I took a drink with Sanchez. He had recommended a new café, the Alcala. Again we found ourselves speaking of Federico who seemed to be making a stir in town. He was entertaining at various cafes with his songs and also being made welcome in the better houses at Bib-Rambla and the Plaza Campillo. I was amused to hear of his latest poem which he presents as a puppet show. It is called The Butterfly and the Spider. It is said he does the voices and acts in both parts.

"A strange title," I remarked. "A curious imagination! There is no doubt he is a most unusual boy."

"Perhaps it is an allegory," said Sanchez. "Political. The butterfly is the progressive, colourful species seeking sunshine and a happy time, while the spider is tradition, trapped in its own dark web, the strands of the bad old days!"

I laughed. "You intellectuals make too much of it."

"We will see which way the wind blows. We have so many changes of Government it could become a hurricane!"

After further consideration of the political theatre it was time for me to go. "Musn't keep Sophia waiting," I said. "She has promised a birthday supper for me tonight, it should be a surprise. Adios, my good friend!"

As I made my way home I knew my supper would not really be a surprise, but it would be different. Sophie was to prepare a dish she said her mother used to make. It was rojoes a moda do Minho. A stew of pork in a pot of wine, lemon and garlic. I found Sophia in the kitchen slicing a lemon and some olives. There was a good smell of garlic. A surprise I had not expected was to find a nest of singing birds. But there was no singing. They were seated round the table, six of them. Sophia, pointing with her knife recited "Teresa, Rosario, Carmen, Maria, Mari and Alicia." It was a pretty sight.

"Boas noches, senoras!"

They nodded politely, but it was clear to me that they were not visiting for my birthday. They were silent, without motion as if made of stone. Sophia put down her knife, made a face and signalled with her eyes, a glance I could not understand. The air was like thunder. Sophia said quietly "Bad news. Poor Alicia."

The women were all friends of Sophia. Three of them were the mothers of children at the school. and Alicia, the red headed one, was often in our house. Carmen and Mari I did not know. Teresa, the daughter of the woman who kept the flower shop near the cathedral I recognised and it was she who finally spoke.

"Alicia, it is only between us, no one else. We will not tell."

Alicia shook her head. I saw her eyes and realised that she had been weeping.

Sophia got to her feet and going to Alicia she put her arms round her.

"It is alright *carino mio*, Luis will not say. I will not say. It is private."
And she kissed her on her forehead. Then she signalled that the
women should leave. They stood and each in turn gave Alicia a
comfort. Some gave a kiss. Then they all filed out without a word
taking Alicia with them. It was clear, something very bad had hurt
the girl.

"It is a tragedy for the whole family. Terrible! Alicia's older sister,
you see. Two days ago she was to be married, but to the surprise and
dismay of the family she did not appear at the church. The guests
waited. It was then found that the bride at the last minute had run
away with a lover. No one knows who it might be. Some say it was
a cousin or distant relation, others believe a gypsy or a cattleman.
Everyone has their own story but the truth is not known!"

I was amazed. Sophia was deeply troubled. I wanted to go to her but
she pushed me away.

"Now it is too late. The bridegroom went to find where the couple
had gone. They were hiding in the forest. He discovered them and
shot the man, also at the same moment wounding Alicia's sister, and
now she might die!"

This was terrible. I had heard nothing of it. It was a tragedy for
Alicia and even more it was a disgrace for the whole family, and
I understood that we should not speak of it. "We will not tell," I
said, "but the talk will spread in the cafes, nothing can prevent it."

Sophia nodded. "Of course." And then my dear wife could not control her tears. She rose from the table and was weeping. I took her
in my arms but she would not be consoled. Alicia was her best
friend. She was loved by all the girls. In their homes there would be
great anger, and there was nothing to be done. I could not enjoy my
birthday. Sophia said she would not eat, and I also. I had brought a
bottle of wine from the Alcala to have with her special supper.
I opened it and brought two glasses. We drank to the last drop.

Some days later I heard that Federico was not always attending the university, and was spending much time with the gypsies. He was also to be found in the cafes, playing and singing, and even with the cattle men by the Genil. With him was Juan, the handsome gypsy from the caves who was a dancer and who had a fine voice. I said to Sophia that she should no longer be unhappy for Alicia. These things happen and if we knew the truth we would find they were not so uncommon. "We will be more cheerful, Sophia. We will not live under the shadow of sadness always looking back. We can do better. I have a suggestion for you. Soon we have a public holiday. We can take four days, and go to the coast. You would like that?"

There was the beginning of a smile. So, we arranged accordingly, and in due time we took the road to the Sierra, gazing up to the high snow and the Pico Veleta. It was a hard journey up the long pass, and at the summit we came to a halt. I had thought we were alone, but no, there was a party of students and my former tutor from the university, Professor Jorge Aragon! The wind was strong in our faces and our voices were tumbling in the cold gusts.

"A magnificent spectacle," shouted the professor. "It is a famous view!"

I knew it. Our breath was taken and we shouted our agreement. Below the steep slopes lay the forests, the woodlands and villages, some with small orchards of apple, cherry and lemons, and above them the birds circling. To the east were the Alpujarra hills, deep ravines and the gentler slopes bright with orange and lemon trees. The Professor said it was a vista never to be forgotten, and be immediately gave us a lesson as if we too were his students.

"Eight hundred years ago, on these stones, in this very lonely place stood the last Moor, a prince, to leave Granada for the last time. His name was Boabdil. He turned to look back and far away was the great Alhambra. He gazed upon it and in his grief he wept many tears. Imagine the sadness of his leaving such a palace. For him, it was a Heaven that had been his home with its memories of generations of his kinsmen. And now? Defeat and the loss of all he loved. Such sadness you could not imagine. That is why this road is called *La Cuesta de las Lagrimas*. A place of tears."

With the students we looked again to the distant palace, its high walls and towers floating on the horizon like a ship borne upon green waves. It was a sight to touch the heart and bruise the imagination. We were sad, but then rejoiced. We were leaving, but only for a few days. We would return to our home which was not so far from those ancient walls. We did not weep. But then, alas, the clouds descended and Granada was covered in darkness. Distant thunder rolled. We could see no more and I told Sophia we should now continue our journey. Before we left "Jorge!" I cried. "*Buena!*" That was a good lecture! I must put it in the journal I am writing. Now we must go!"

He replied that we should do so, and he added "Detail, Luis ! Remember detail! For all you are putting in your book. You must devise some ideas! Use the imagination the good Lord gave to you." He grinned. "You can use fiction as well as fact which, I fear, is what all you schoolmasters do these days!"

His last words died on a shout of wind. But, while I did not agree with him I did not forget them, and again I became impatient to return to writing of the world that opened around me.

What would it be? It has been said that my Espana is a country too much in love with Death. I do not entirely believe that. As I always tell Sophia my country is more like the corrida. It is a land of sol y sombre, of sun and shade. That is what I think. It is a place of shadows as well as songs. There is death of course. There could not be life without it. But, not all is sadness. There is music and laughter in our homes and in the cafes. That, I told myself, was a better thought as we turned our faces to the south.

We took our way, descending slowly to the coast to find an ocean as blue as the sky. Our lodging house in a small garden was not so comfortable but it was only for three nights. The first evening, at a

Tapas we were surprised to find two Guardia Civil leaning against the Bar and I supposed they had taken too much to drink for they were shouting and cursing. I listened intently for, to my surprise, I heard one of them mention the name of Lorca. His companion took a big gulp from his glass and mumbled "Do not talk to me of that soft boy, he has not the balls of a broken bull!"

"He learns his songs from the gitano," responded his fellow drunk. "And who understands them? You cannot, but I can and will do better. I am to be a poet you know!"

"You are a bastard! You lie! And I am laughing! You cannot put two words in one line!"

"And you, my son are as weak as a kid who cannot suck his mother's tits!"

Holding to the Bar rail and swaying from side to side he continued "I tell you my song. Hum?" He then chanted "Guardia Civil under a burning sky, where is my brandy for I thirst or die? The good Lord made it water and I pray it should be blood of the Blessed Mary. Now the blood in my veins is sweet as Brandy wine, and we must weep, and we are afraid, for already the hungry crocodile approaches to devour the infidel!"

His companion, very red in the face shouted "Ill begotten pig you are *idiota*, and you say that only to make me mad! Here is one for you!" And swinging his fist he made a dangerous lunge at his companion. This was very bad. I leapt to my feet and I would have seized the aggressor had not Sophia pulled me away. "NO Luis! NO! You will be arrested!"

She was right. I had not stopped to consider. I cooled down but was amazed that those appointed to keep the peace should fight among themselves and have so many drunken words under their hat. They should not fight like dogs. And what could they know about Lorca? Meantime, the 'poet', sliding to the floor, raised his glass and with tears on his face whispered "Senor! Amigo! To the King!" Then he passed out smiling as if he had found his promised land. Sophia was angry and said I was foolish to try to stop the men fighting. But I feared it was a bad omen. If men of the Guardia Civil stood against each other, what danger might there be for the ordinary citizen. I thought again of the two gypsies at the caves who were supposed to be brothers but who so easily set against each other.

I was thankful that the remainder of our little holiday passed in peace. We found some refreshment in the villages along the coast beside the quiet sea and were enchanted by the beauty of the long shore. There were small farms, but Sophia was most interested in the single boat fishermen of which there were many. She wished to compare them with those of her native Portugal who were rich from a great variety of fish that they caught, including sole, sea bream, tuna and the octopus which they trapped in the alcatruz, the earthenware pot that is lowered to the seabed.

"Someday," Sophia said "we may go to my country and I will show you the coast which is also rich in the building of ships of every kind."

Our little holiday was ended too soon, and we set our faces to the north and the return by the high sierra. We would go beside the ridges of the Alpujarra hills, by the woodland, the orchards of cherry, lemons and the almond trees, by the parched scrub land, the Sierra de la Contraviesa and along the route the warrier Moors took all those many centuries ago.

I returned to the classroom. It is often said that in my country's psyche there is a sadness that cannot be explained, and when it comes it freezes the heart and damages the spirit. It's voice is heard in the flamenco singing. Who can understand it? The dancing of the girls is often so beautiful, there is such passion and such grace in the *baile* and the *zapateado*, so rapid like a rifle shot. I have known the *compas* (rhythms) since a child but it does not help. For reasons I do not know a sadness took hold of me. I was not sick, but I remembered the poor Guardia Civil who thought he was a poet.

After struggling with work for my boys in class it was my custom to go down to a café find some refreshing conversation. I called at the Mirador but there was no one. At the Alcala I discovered an unexpected gathering and to my surprise, in deep conversation was Federico. I grasped his hand and greeted him warmly.

"Well, you have been busy Federico! I hear that you are playing and singing everywhere. What happened to your studies with the Law?"

He laughed. "That was the fault of my father. He said I should do it. But The Law is not for me. I think the piano lessons my mother gave me were the tyrant from the beginning. They grabbed hold of me. Music is always in my blood!"

I said his father would not be pleased, but he paid no heed. He took my arm. "Come and sit, you must meet my new friend the musician, we are considering a composition for my puppet show. Here is Manuel, you may not know it but he has great ability!" He was growing excited and began to shout "Hey musician you are a magician, we will have fun!" Confidentially he added "In Paris he was exclusive to art and music and he had the great pleasure of discussions with Ravel and also Debussy, and in Madrid he has much to do, maybe it will be opera. I am a lucky fellow! Together we will perhaps arrange some plays with music!"

A tall, slim man of serious aspect rose and took my hand. "Federico exaggerates, do not believe him! I am pleased to meet you."

A gypsy maid came fussing round. More drinks were ordered, and she was glad to have the money. There were others joining us and I was introduced to several men who Federico insisted were poets and musicians, and among them was Juan from the *cuevas* who kindly remembered me. Such interest was now removing my sadness like clouds passing from the sun and it was even better when Sanchez Carvajal, my newspaper friend, appeared. I thought he should be in his office.

"You are in dangerous company," he grinned. "Shall we take a walk, or these lads will make you sing for your supper!"

We took a turn round the plaza and Sanchez said "They are clever artists and often as attractive as orioles that fly in the sierra but sometimes I feel they are too much in love with each other." His face clouded. "I hope this is not so, but you know how it is with theatre people, always a fiesta, a parade, a song, and such affection may go too far."

I said I was sure there was no danger of that. I would not believe it.

"My friend I hope you are right. He paused to consider, then added "Is it not strange that celebrations should transpire when the political scene is so heavy throughout the land. You may have heard the Government is now allowing the import of large quantities of wheat from America?"

This was so typical of Sanchez! I had to smile. "Is that not good?"

"It means trouble. In the bad lands there is drought, with a poor harvest. Most of our farmers cannot compete. They have little to sell, so you can see the difficulty? They are suffering and accusing the Government for not helping them. Many may lose their land and then with no business they could even starve. Who would help them?"

"Surely, that will not be allowed to happen?"

"The problem is not simple. Those who make more wine than corn may be safe, also olives and perhaps oranges for export. But on many farms that is not possible and disaster will follow. In the north there are good exports of steel, iron and copper, and that is good for the families there. Many are becoming rich. But the farmers are not so fortunate. They see what is happening and they are even more angry. In their situation I think it is understandable."

"Sanchez, please! You are making me depressed again! And just when I was being happy with Federico and that other fellow, the musician."

"I am sorry you are sad, I do not mean to upset you. You mention Manuel. You know who he is? It is Manuel de Falla for whom, it is said, there can be a big future. Imagine! Cadiz can produce artists! That is a good sign."

I needed a good sign. And another drink. Sanchez proposed we should go to his office. There he said he kept a bottle or two of brandy. It would cheer me up and he could show me some private reports he had received. The office of Sanchez was amusing, like a fish tank with walls of glass so that he could perceive the work floor below where type was being set, also the printing machines. From a cupboard he produced two glasses and a bottle. He smiled. "I do not often provide this, it is only for a friend or a celebration. But today," he paused dramatically, "no celebration."

I asked why, and he replied his newspaper would be reporting how the Army had put down a general strike in Catalunia and imprisoned the strike leaders. "But now the Army has turned against itself. Many officers are angry because their pay is not enough and they will not stop the killing and disorder. The peasants and workers are coming together more and more and joining UGT and CNT, the Union General de Trabadores and the Conferacion Nacional de Trabajo."

Hardly a celebration, I agreed. It was depressing, and for a few moments we drank in silence. Then I remarked how fortunate we were in Granada where all was at peace.

That is good," he replied. "But you cannot be too optimistic. You see what is happening to the larger estates, the rich ones? Even here in Andalusia land is being taken in protest, it is said, by Bolsheviks! If that is true there will be still more anger."

He added that he sometimes wished to be in the north, the Asturias where the miners prospered with their steel and iron. "There are rich families up there who have become the envy even of our friends in Catalunia!"

I did not wish to argue with my kind host. I was drinking his brandy. But I did not believe he would really care to leave Granada, his home, and mine. The most beautiful city in the world.

✳✳✳

It was when I became Director of my school that I made the decision. I would not continue with my journal. Number one, I had to spend much more time at work with new responsibilities, and number two, why should I write only sadness, and the difficulties my country was facing? It was enough to know it. This I explained to my friend Sanchez and his pretty wife Rosa, and Professor Jorge Aragon when they came for *comida* (supper) which Sophia had planned as a celebration for my promotion. She had taken time to produce a *paella* with the best food — *calasparra* rice, fresh *pollo* and *gambas* with *pimiento, cebollas, chorizo, garlik, tomates, guisantes, aceitunas,* and much more. There was applause for this big dish, but not for my decision. Jorge said "Luis you must find time to continue the writing. I believe this, you can do it."

"That is what I tell him," added Sophia. "If he is not writing he becomes sad and I do not want a sad man to live with!"

Rosa clapped her hands and agreed. "It is your responsibility Luis. After all, this Lorca is stirring waves and could become a proud tribute to Granada." And with a dangerous smile she added "We have seen how you like that young man!"

Sanchez joined the chorus. "There are many who like him. And after all Luis, you told me you have a genuine interest and good hopes for your protégé, so even if there is nothing else good to say you should keep writing to keep his talent in view."

In the end of course it was their words and kindness, and maybe a little too much good wine Jorge had brought, that changed my mind. If I had too much work at school, they would help me. How could I refuse? They would keep me acquainted with such news as I required. If they could do this I decided I would find the time to continue.

※※※

It was Saturday in mid June, the day before the Corrida de Toros. Federico made his way through the plaza to the bullring accompanied by Juan, the gypsy, the one from the cuevas of Sacromonte. The sun above the city created a furnace sufficient to raise blisters on the flesh of even the most hardened, leather-skinned *granjero*. Pushing through the throng of chattering citizens and visitors their aim was to find Paco, the leading banderillo in the pay of the torero Ignacio Sanchez Mejias. They knew Paco would be doing his duty at the *chiqcueros* (pens) to inspect both the bulls and the horses for his master to use in the ring tomorrow afternoon.

Juan had his arm around Federico's shoulder. "Rico, are we not mad? We cannot remain here much longer. We will melt!"

"If you are putting your money on Ignacio we must first find Paco, then we will go."

"I may not put money. It depends not only on Ignacio but what I can find on the horses and the bulls. Are the horses from your father?"

Federico shook his head. "Not from my father. He said there are now many horses imported from America. A special breed. He is interested. I think he will have a place in the box tomorrow at the President's side."

The crowds thickened and around the pens where some of the bulls were herded there was much shouting and sounds of a fight. Federico and Juan pushed through the throng to a nearer set of pens where they had spotted their man.

"There he is!" cried Juan. "Paco! Hola you miserable *hongo!*" (toadstool). "Are you hiding, we could not see you!"

The small, swarthy banderillo thumped Federico on the back and growled "Ah, you guapo hijo of a bitch, you come to help me choose?" He grinned. "You would not know the best toro if it was eating at your table!" And mopping his brow and spitting he added "Muy caliente, eh?"

"Mind your tongue !" warned Juan. "It is not your place to spit on the name of my friend Rico, he is a son of Rodriguez the farmer, an aficionado who can judge a toro and a caballo much better than you!"

They moved to a second pen and pointing to a bull Paco cried "Alright amigo, what do you say about this fine fellow. My boss would like it? His coat is good and I will check the horns."

Before Juan could reply Federico surprisingly said "He is heavy. Too much corn. He would be slow. Looks as if he would weigh almost a ton! I promise you Ignacio is not such a fool as to accept him. With respect I say you should find another two who would weigh less and give a stronger *arrancada.*" (Bull's charge).

"Very good!" exclaimed Paco. "You want my job, eh?"

Federico laughed. "No, no! The pay would not keep me in shirt and shoes!"

They then moved to see the horses. As they were turning away the torero himself, Ignacio Sanchez Mejias, unexpectedly appeared. He was an imposing figure in his white blouse, britches and high boots, and he walked with the easy, assured step of a dancer. Federico shook his hand warmly and bowed.

The torero responded with a smile. "Ah my poetical friend, I trust you will have a prayer for me tomorrow!" With a graceful gesture he added "Has my man chosen well?"

Federico nodded as Paco approached and said "I did not expect to see you here boss, but you will not be disappointed. We have two of the best. But the caballos, not so lucky. All are weak in the leg. Very old. That vaquero, son of a bitch of the street will ask too much, but," he slid his hand across his throat and growled "he may regret it!"

"We will attend to that later," responded Ignacio. "For the moment I would like to see the two you have chosen." Then drawing Ferderico aside and lowering his voice said "Comida, tonight? Los Aarandes, as usual. You could come at eight."

Juan had heard but pretended not to notice. There was the slightest frown on his dark face. An expression difficult to read.

✳✳✳

I decided I should cherish some optimism for my country. The Government's decision to give more attention to education pleased me and other teachers with whom I discussed our condition. However, the situation of the *campesinos* (peasants) in much of Andalusia could not be worse. They could neither read nor write more than their names. Perhaps now they would have some help. For me the good initiative meant that I would have better pay, and a new building for my school could be a possibility. I was much occupied, but I always made time each week to take a walk with Sophia and share our thoughts.

I did not attend the corrida. Several weeks later we took a walk from the Nueva through the Gate of Pomegranites to enjoy the peace of the Court of Myrtles and by the Long Pool to the great gardens. There were not so many people but by chance we came upon none other than Federico. He was sitting alone and in some deep thought. We greeted him. It was a pleasure for we had not seen him for some time.

"Hola Federico! We have missed you. It is a fine day for the gardens. Did you find a seat at the last corrida?"

He nodded.

"I have heard it was good with some great performances. Did you enjoy it?"

Coming out of his thinking he stood up. "Si! Mucho!" And he added "Ignacio was the most popular. Magnifico! The crowd rose to him. For his second toro he was on his knees with the muleta very still, like Joselito, and had no fear. He is heroico!"

Sophia said "We have not seen you. I thought you must be away somewhere."

"Well, I was in the Conservatory. Piano. And then with other students and Professor Aragon I made some visits in the campo to various towns, also to Cordoba, Sevilla and to Huelva. It was great!"

He was excited about the visit. His irrepressible gaiety was infectious, it gathered you in as if he had injected a magic potion into your veins that held you captive and created pictures in you mind.

"We travelled as far as Vallodolid, I had not been there before. Of course it was famous, for here Isabella of Castile was married to King Ferdinand. Also Columbus died in the city and Cervantes house was there it was informative, I wished to have remained there much longer. Now, I have written my experiences."

This was a surprise because I did not think he wrote his poems or songs but always recited them like an actor. He had not been taught as an actor in the teatro but had an ability for the stage that seemed in-born and quite natural.

"You have written a book?" I exclaimed. "Bravo ! You are intending to publish?"

He frowned. "I am not sure. But, I hope."

Sophia clapped her hands. "You must do it Federico! I have heard your songs and stories. We enjoy them. It is good that you put them in a book. Many people here in Granada would want to have it, that is sure."

"Not so much songs," he replied, "My book will be about the campo, describing many places. It is like opening one door to a garden, and then another to a garden, and many more. I made some drawings."

I asked what he would call his book. He shrugged. "It could be 'Landscapes in Andalusia and Castile. My impressions."

"Federico, I always said you were my best student, and here is the proof! Is it not so, Sophia?"

She agreed and added that she was sure the Professor would be pleased if he made a book.

"We have a little time," I said, "Let us walk together." I took Federico's arm. "Look how fine it is Sophia! So clear we can view the snow on the sierra." I told Federico we had taken a journey that way through the hills and to the sea.

He nodded. "My papa has a house there. When I was very young we had holidays to escape the heat. We had such sun as we are now having this summer. But I do not care to go. I have found I cannot work there. The sea is bright, but for me it is a fearful mystery with shadows I dare not enter."

I did not know what he meant and I was even more puzzled when he said they were the shadows of his tears.

Part Two

Rain on a Parched Land

Manuel de Falla was never too busy to meet with Lorca who, he affirmed, was a good friend. I knew that they were often together with Juan the gypsy, drinking at the Alcala, for I also visited that café. There were other poets and artists who gathered there. It could be noisy and, inevitably, there was much conversation and also argument concerning new directions in writing and music. Manuel was often quiet and withdrawn, but sometimes he liked to counsel Federico as if he was his protégé. He declared "There will always be cynics, and many may not understand. But do not be discouraged, Federico. You have a natural ear for music. You have skill with the guitarra, and also, the piano. The city needs you. It has been losing its love for flamenco, is that not so, Juan? I know Federico loves flamenco. Together we should give some encouragement, perhaps make a play for the theatre. What do you say, Juan?"

Juan agreed. "Very good! We should do it. This is my idea. We take the bullring! In place of toros we will have a romaria, a celebration of dancing! My people would like it, and perhaps many others too!"

Federico laughed, then pulled a face. "I think that is going too far."

"Come Rico, that is not like you!" said Manuel. "Even the poorest *campesino* has his songs. You know, when wealthy clever-clever idiots turn their back on you I tell them not to use their brains on your songs but simply to let the words fall like rain on a parched land. I advise - let them encompass your heart with love, with joy, with sadness, let them dissolve the hard rock that does not forgive, and allow the flowers to appear. Listen to the flowers I tell them! They can inform your poor mind. They are servants to the words of the

35

poet which arrive like a prayer, an angel. They are the unexpected visitor at your door."

"Ole!" cried Lorca. "You should make poems and I will play the music!"

That is not, of course, what happened, but their friendship was close and I could see their talents could marry together. And they did. But Federico proved also to be a very accomplished solo performer. He gave a remarkable public lecture, a talk to a mixed audience in the Conservatory. His theme was 'Deep Song', an attempt to explain that moment in creative art that reached to the centre, the truth, a kind of perfection. It was strongly but not exclusively Andalusian, and it sprang from a compulsive obsession with love, passion, despair and above all the knowledge and acceptance of death. The gypsies understood very well, for this magic, elusive and never certain, was to be found in a state of being that Federico called Duende. Its heart was often found in flamenco, and in singing and musical performance but only if a kind of emotive perfection, perhaps a single moment, was born. It was the soul of Espana.

I took Sophia with me to that lecture. It was well received, if not totally understood, and in due course it gave rise to an unexpected event. The word had got round the city, from the cafes and restaurants to the university and many private homes that the following Saturday there was to be a special performance in the bullring by permission of the Mayor and Council. In this instance the occasion had nothing to do with the corrida. It was here that Manuel and Federico decided to work on a celebration of the cante jondo (the deep song).

With Juan's help they asked the gitanos to leave their tableo in Sacromonte late on the Saturday after sundown and prepare to perform in the city. Several needed little persuasion. They included Francisco Cameron and Jose Manuel Lopez with their guitarras, and four girls who came in their brightest silks and cottons, and their gold combs and earrings. Clara, Sylvia, Nina and Maria were to dance flamenco. There would be songs too, of which the words of some were ancient enough to know of no beginning, and others which seemed to look into lives lived today. Federico said "In our songs we try to reveal the soul of Andalusia."

On that Saturday the event resembled a theatrical performance with jostling, laughing and expectant Granadinos packed behind the barrera and in the higher seats from which cushions were often thrown at a poor torero who they found was not *valiente*. (brave). A small wooden floor and several chairs had been placed in the centre of the ring and around the sides a blaze of torches sent sparks and smoke up to the darkening sky. A bugle sounded, but there was no President in his box waving a white handkerchief. Instead there was the Mayor and Manuel de Falla waving to the crowds below.

With Sophia at my side, just behind the barrera, my view was clear and I could hear the tuning of the guitarra on the still air. Juan, who had worked hard making the arrangements, came to join us. For Sophia he explained the action. "In your country I do not think the music is the same. Here we have many dances. The Tango and Rumba of course, but also Alegrias, Seguiriya and Bulerias. The compas are 4-4 in Tangos and Rumbas, 3-4 for Fandangos, but there are 12 beats in flamenco. You follow?"

Sophia said she was not sure. "But, like a good student I will attend!"

As the gypsies entered the ring the loyal audience clapped and cheered. The performers waited for silence, a dramatic pause in the stillness of the air before the first notes sprang from the guitarras and a throaty call like an agony escaped from a pair of lips as if to awaken the dancers to life. One twirled her way on to the wooden floor and with arms raised she began a brilliant zapateado across the rhythm of the strings. Tak-tak-tikka-tikka tak-tika-tak-tak went her feet as she arched her back and sent her scarlet skirt swirling like a flame blown by the wind. Her fingers snapped like castanets, accenting a different compas of beats and rhythm. The three other waiting dancers, Sylvia, Nina and Maria began their palmas which gave a signal to the audience. Row upon row we all began to clap, accompanying the zapateado. There were cries of "Ole!" as Clara, the principal dancer, thrust her bare arms to the stars, and twirled her hips, sliding left and right, teasing as if boldly inviting a lover to come to her. No one came. The lover was the insistent strumming of the two guitarras and the violent, passionate cries one minute wounding the night air and the next promoting a savage joy. There was a sense of triumph and loss, and I could not separate the two.

When Clara ended her performance there was a sudden silence then a roar as, row upon row, we stood to applaud. As the cries died away Federico stepped from the shadows. He introduced the three remaining dancers, one clad in scarlet, one in rose and the third in white and gold. They performed, each in turn, showing their individual style. We clapped and stamped and cheered. One of the musicians played solo guitarra and accompanied his companion who began to chant and sing with a high, plaintive voice in Calo, the ancient gypsy language which few understood.

"Tree of lemon and flower, sweet oleander, my heart bids me find the rose. But the moon has cut it with a thousand knives, the sand is black with blood and the bells of the sheep ring out in the sadness of my tortured dream."

There was more dancing, then Federico stepped forward again to applause like the breaking of an ocean wave. We, the citizens of Granada, wanted to show our appreciation. He answered with a song about the cattlemen of the Genil. For my Sophia the event may not have found that hidden moment called duende, but it was a new and startling experience. And for me? I could not help but applaud. Flamenco had returned to Granada.

What had begun so well now continued elsewhere. There was more flamenco. In the plaza La Mimbre near the Alhambra

Federico and de Falla produced another Concurso del Cante Jondo. On this occasion it included a competition of traditional music and dance. The men wore ancient dress. Each had first to sing solo, they then had to sing and play the guitarra. After that they had to play solo guitarra, then sing again with *palmas* and *zapateado* and dance once more. Juan took part and was accorded a rose. But it was said no one could beat Tio Tenazas from Sevilla who became famous throughout the land, unless it was Manuel Salamanca. I had heard his name before but not in flamenco. He was a master jeweller from Cordoba.

The performance by the gitane, the music and the dancing, had made me feel proud to be a Grenadino with the privilege of teaching the history and traditions of Andalusia. But the occasion which brought such joy to my heart was hurt by a growing alarm. For apart from the troubles in the north, and the selfishness of Catalunia, Jose Canalejas, who had taken the reins of government from Maura, was reported killed by an anarchist, or so it was said. There was a rumour that he would be succeeded by Prieto and Alba who were Liberals. I felt there was a chance that they might settle the unrest but, my friend Sanchez with whom I discussed these matters said I was mistaken.

"You have only to look at Catalunia. The *rabassaires*, the wine families, are still making trouble, demanding better terms for their work, and even here, Luis, things are becoming bad for us as well!"

That I could not understand, but he continued "I will tell you one thing. It is fortunate that Federico's family left the farm and took that new house down the Recogidas. You know as well as I that the *campesinos* are not simply grumbling, they are now making serious trouble. You can hardly blame them!"

I had heard that some important landowners were disappearing. Many were going to the cities, and some even leaving the country. Their properties were being taken by anarchists. In the weeks that followed there was violence and rioting by farm workers who joined

together in their hatred of government officials, the Army and even
the Church. They had suffered long enough from the greed of the
fortunate few. Poor harvests had made the situation worse and
many families down on the Vega were facing starvation. Sanchez
said his newspaper was reporting terrible stories from the lands
around villages and towns. Olvera, Loja, Osuna, Carmona and
many more. Nothing was sure as anarchy stalked the land. A new
Government, devised by Eduardo Dato, closed the Cortes, and
the socialists made wild statements shouting down the monarchy,
calling for a seven-hour working day, abolishment of the Army,
separation of Church and State and the closure of monasteries.
The class difference flared more acutely than ever before with
Labour openly fighting Capital. Politicians of all colours were
under threat and some were even murdered. Who would not be
alarmed? I was finding it difficult to concentrate on my work, and
I could see that Sophia was worrying. It was not like her to be
depressed but she reported that she had seen some children from
the country who were ill clad and near to starving. "It is terrible,
Luis," she said. "I am worried for them, and their families, they
have so little to eat."

Happily, not all was bad news. The long English war had drawn to
an end with the Germans surrendering after many bloody battles.
Also, the book Federico had written about his travels was published
and it was said people were looking to buy it. It was not surprising
that a celebration happened at the Alcala with his friends. I was not
there but I hoped to get a copy of the book. As it turned out I was
given one by Dona Vicenta. I think she was becoming quite fond of
me! She called me down to the new house and I was offered a glass
of wine. She asked if I had read the book and when I confessed that
I had not she kindly gave me a copy.

"You should have it please, you were his teacher and are a good
friend."

"Well ma'am, Federico is becoming successful and is now well
known and admired. I think he will be teaching ME!"

"I too am impressed by what he has done," she replied. "And although he will not admit it I think his father is quite proud of him." With an unexpected wink she added "It is because when the book sells it earns some money! Maybe not much but it is pleasing to my husband. And I must tell you the latest of what my admired son has done. Here we have a small orchard and he has now planted cypress trees there. He says it is a protection for the house and will shelter him from all political talk, the anger and the problems we have."

There was certainly plenty of talk, and even some alarm. We spoke briefly of the troubles for a government that could no longer govern and Dona Vicenta said "my husband believes there could be more violence." Then, changing the unpleasant subject she spoke again of Federico.

"Perhaps you will give me your advice, Senor Castejou. Federico tells us his professor of Art is encouraging him to go to the Residencia de Estudiantes in Madrid. The University. You would agree this might be good for him?"

I had not thought of it, but replied that his professor would know if such a move would be useful to him. While I had no experience of the Residencia I supposed it could do no harm. I said "I imagine there will be artists at the Residencia and that might be a good climate for him. After all, he already enjoys his time here with de Falla and the others at the Alcala, and perhaps it is time for him to make a change and study more academic work as well as continuing with his poetry."

Dona Vicenta smiled. "Yes, that is good. I believe he should now go to live in the Residencia. You would give him your blessing?"

I said that I would, and to myself I thought this was a very sensible lady.

"Now mister teacher," she said "together we will drink for his success!" She raised her glass. "I am pleased you are such a good friend of my son!"

✳✳✳

It was Sophia who said what I already knew, that you could not be known as an admired writer unless your work was published in a book that was available to all and which sold many copies. "But," she added, "I am told Lorca does not do this. He has many songs but not in a book. He is clever, so why does he not do it? He has made only one book, and it does not have his poems."

I had given this some thought and I had an answer. "Sophia, *querido*, I can tell you why. He always wants his poems to be spoken, or sung, and then they become alive. He does not want his words to be in a closed book. You have heard him sing and recite his poetry, and it is successful because not only does he like music, he likes to perform as you have seen. I knew it was so even when he was very young. He is like an actor who wants the words spoken aloud, and he can do it very well."

We were discussing this with a member of the group of friends and writers who Federico regularly met at the Alcala. His name was Luis Rosales, a charming fellow, also a poet and whose family lived near the university in Calle Duquesa. He said that he also remembered Federico as a kid. "Yes, he liked to dress up and play the part of different people. Once I saw him pretending to be a *sacerdote* (priest) giving a sermon. He was *malo* but very funny and he made me laugh!"

"So he is not religious?" asked Sophia.

Rosales said he thought he was not very religious but, by nature, very superstitious. "I can give you an example. He said at his father's home, Huerta de San Vicente which you must know, there have come some birds, but not the usual little thrush or buntings, they are falcons or vultures and they perch in the garden, on the roof, even at the windows, and that, he told me, means they bring bad luck to the house." Rosales shrugged. "I think it very strange, but it is not a joke. He is serious."

I could not believe this. "Surely it is just his imagination, perhaps a dream. A falcon is a bird of prey. It is quite common in the sierra, very high around the Pico de Veleta where I know there are vultures and kestrels. I have seen them there riding the wind. That is where they live. I doubt if they would ever visit a city!"

Rosales said he hoped I was right. "I told Federico we do not need bad luck, he should forget the birds. Instead I told him he should sing like a bird! He has a good voice!"

Sophia laughed "But you must also persuade him to put his songs in a book."

"We are always telling him," said Rosales, "but he does not listen!"

✳✳✳

I felt sad that Federico would go to the Residencia in Madrid because we would not see him in Granada with the gitanos. For a time he was with de Falla and again performing. They had discovered a hall behind the Teatro Isabel and as well as flamenco they were making short plays which were said to be most amusing. But, of course, I had to admit it was good that he should go to the Residencia and attend the university. He said to me that he felt lucky, because his family had agreed to pay the fees. Also, Jorge Aragon, his Professor, said he would be visiting Madrid University and, as he put it, he would keep a careful eye.

After two months Dona Vicenta came one day to my house to say she had some news. I was pleased to see her again.

"He is a good son," she said smiling. "I told Federico must write to me each week. I did not think he would, but now I have a letter! You would like to hear it?"

I answered that I would be very interested. I had been missing him and I hoped he was well.

"Yes, very well! He writes — *'Here is my new home. Surprising! The Residencia is central near Palacio de Mondoa, the Prime Minister's place. It is fifteen minutes from Madrid centre by tramcar. The great parque is also near but not so fine as our Generalife. In the residence there are more than 100 etudients, and there are gardens which remind me of home because there are poplar trees and many flowers, roses, iris and oleander. Some etudients are studying medicine, also engineering. For most subjects there are tutors. There is a library, a salon for music and a common room. I am very happy because I will find many friends here, even artists.*

The barrio also is exciting, I am exploring. There is a zoo but I hate this. In place of the bears and monkeys on view there we should put the Prime Minister! We have a song — Dotty dotty Dato do, in the Zoo you have to go, Take your Ministers, macaco, THEY are monkeys as we know! Also every Nationalista and his brother and his sister, Lock them in the cage so we, the artists, can be free. In Espana WE will rule, a lesson that we learned at school!'

I could not refrain from laughing, nor could Dona Vicenta. "You think," she gasped, dabbing her eyes, all poets are mad?"

"Not Federico, ma'am, I fear it is not our poets, it is the politicians who have lost their heads!"

"No, Senor Castejou. Not all. It would be a disaster! But, I am very pleased my son is happy!"

In a later letter, more sensibly, Federico praised the Residencia. *'The furniture is not so good, but practical. The place is very clean, but my bed is hard. It is a separate world, but international, and we have visitors from different countries. Some call here to lecture. I have met H.G. Wells, Chesterton, also Belloc and Ravel.'*

He had a comfortable double study in which to sleep and work which he was sharing with Luis Bunuel. *'He came here before me and is older, studying Natural Science and Philosophy.'* Federico wrote that he did not compose the stupid song about Dato but added that he had almost finished writing a play, his first serious drama which was exciting him and which, he hoped, would be staged at Madrid's Teatro Eslava.

When I told this to Sophia she considered it was a natural thing for him to do. "I often think he should be an actor, he has a presence that is so strong, he is quite handsome, and when he speaks his poems, or sings, the air trembles, and so do my friends! You know this? They say he is very *provocatevo!*"

"And you think so, too?"

She blushed and for a moment did not know how to reply. "Well, he would be a cheerful husband I think, he has so much laughter in him!"

"Then you are in love with him as well?"

"Luis, you are teasing! Don't be foolish, you know I love you only!"

"But, I am not so cheerful?"

"You are macho! That is what I like."

I felt suddenly, and strongly, that this conversation should not go further and became rather sad. I confessed to Sophia that I would miss Federico very much, for my journal was more and more occupied with him. But again I thought to stop writing it, for how could I continue if he disappeared? My Sophia disagreed and demanded that I should be more intelligent.

"He has not disappeared! I am sure Federico will come to his family in the vacatione and we will see him then. Granada is the true home he loves. Here he belongs to everybody, to his friends in the café and the homes where he is popular with his singing, and the piano." She turned from me and murmured "He does not belong only to you."

I fell silent. I knew what she was saying, and what she felt. We had no child. We could not have children. Federico's existence was a constant reminder to me, and to her. I believe she thought I was making him the son we could not have. She became upset. I went to her and took her in my arms and I was bitter that someone, anyone, even such a one as Federico could interrupt my life with sadness and the darkness like a shadow that followed me, that was in my footsteps wherever I went. Sophia was stronger than I. She did not cry or make a scene. We kissed. "Promise me you will continue with your writing? After all, even if you do not see Federico we will hear his news, The Lorca family is friendly to us, and so is Federico's professor. And Sanchez also."

Women! What is the use of arguing?

Making a face and pretending to be angry she continued "If you say no I will never again make you a supper of Gaspacho a Alentejana!"

I was on my knees in a pretending prayer.

"And I will never make you Frango na Pucara!"

Even worse! Unlike the macho man she said I was, I gave in. "Yes, yes!" I cried. "Alright! For you I will try!"

That evening, in peace and calm, together we made the Gaspacho. My favourite dish. And the Frango in a pot followed. With a bottle of good wine.

"To your journal!" she smiled in victory, raising her glass. I raised my glass to her. "Gracias!" How could she know my writing, however poor, was, and always would be, the rescue boat from which I would sink or swim.

✳✳✳

"Luis Bunuel," said Federico, "with respect I must ask you not to bring her to our room. She is *prostituta* and you know as well as

I that no woman is allowed in the Residencia, that is the rule. If you continue to go with her you will please find another place."

"Another place be damned!" replied Bunuel. "There is no other place!"

"You can take her to the *parque*. What you want with her I cannot think. I know it is not my business, but I have work to do, Luis. And, I am writing. If you wish to be with her, good luck, but please keep her away!"

The argument continued, not in bitterness, although Federico was plainly upset. Finally, Bunuel agreed to move out and Federico found another student to take his place in the shared room. His name was Emilio Aladren, a young artist studying to become a sculptor. He showed interest in Federico's writing and especially the play which was almost complete.

Emilio thought 'The Butterfly's Evil Spell' was an odd title for a play, but Federico would not change it. He said "It is a serious story, an experiment, and can be interpreted in different ways. It will open new directions for the drama."

※※※

Emilio started the search. He was sensitive and compassionate by nature and was concerned because Federico had left the Residencia in the evening and had not returned. Other students, including another poet called Rafael Alberti were also puzzled and it was he who, in the end, discovered Federico sitting alone on a bench in the parque.

"Federico! At last! We have been looking for you all night. What mischief are you up to? Emilio said your bed was empty."

"Not as empty as me!"

He was clearly distressed, and getting to his feet he started to pace to and fro.

"Come on Federico you must be starving! Best get back. Breakfast will be gone."

"I am not hungry! And I tell you this, it would not happen in Granada!" He sounded very angry. "What kind of people are these in Madrid! They do not deserve a theatre, they have no understanding. Whores and wooden-headed butchers! The *campesino* in the meanest village would understand, so what is it with these grand people of the city? I damn them, I curse them!"

It appeared that the Butterfly's Evil Spell on stage had caused nothing but derision among the theatre-goers. Worse still, the critics had pronounced it to be rubbish. After four performances the play was removed. Federico's disappointment was a deep wound. The Butterfly was the first serious play he had attempted and his effort had ended in disaster. For days he had few words for anyone except Emilio who shared his room and who did his best to disperse his friend's gloom.

"Listen, Federico, why not make a change, you are getting too close to your work. I know it myself. My work begins at the drawing board and is linear, but also I am concerned with form, exploration of the human form, three dimensions and I have to give it a rest. Bunuel told me change your clothes. That is how he put it. He said go to the cinema. Anything. I think that is what I should do. And you should come with me."

For several days the *barrio*, (the city centre), became their playground. Luis Bunuel joined them. They had no inclination to sample the new dance clubs, but they found some amusement in the cinema, visiting the Olympia, and also made the first of many visits to the Prado. Step by step Federico's black mood was dissolving and a new interest caught his attention. The Cibeles Fashion Week was causing a stir. It was as if Paris had come to make Madrid a la mode, observed Emilio. Federico was equally attracted and they talked their way into several of the fashion events. Miguel Marinero was showing and raising applause for his long black gowns worn over a red dress and accompanied by accessories including necklaces of pearls hanging down to the waist. There were jaunty hats and calf length boots. Jesus Lorenzo was showing a fur collection and Juana Martin followed Marinero with his offering called 'The Style of Black.' It was all very *'moderno'*.

Bunuel said he was interested in the production techniques of the shows and decided to go back stage and take a look.

"No, no!" cried Federico, "you cannot, the women will not allow it!"

"Try me!"

Emilio thought it was worth a try, so in the end the three of them introduced themselves as 'students of couture' and, after a little difficulty, and a touch of bribery, succeeded in getting past the stage door keeper. They found the dressing room a near disaster with garments strewn on the floor and the model girls, who were very young, and barely clad, seated beside a long wall mirror. Some were filing their finger nails, others smoking and chatting and taking their ease between exits and entrances. There was a sweet and sour smell of powder, paint and hair spray and womanly perspiration. When a tall. matronly woman who was fully clad spotted the three of them peering round a pile of baskets she shrieked "Mother of Mary! Mother of God! Out, out or I call the Policia!" Bunuel said he thought it would be wise to take her 'advice', and they withdrew. Later, deciding on a modest refreshment at the Café Montana, they mulled over their innocent escapade. Luis Bunuel mysteriously declared that his vision of female beauty would enrich his next essay for the philosophy seminar. Emilio said "If we could have remained there I might have made a drawing. It would be better than those casts in the museo!" Federico found more interest in the fashions which he found attractive but which, he asserted, could only be for the very rich.

In the evenings, if they were not out on the town, the three friends often gathered in the common room of the Residencia to read or discuss the day's disasters or success. One night in Spring their small group was enlarged by other students who had heard that Federico had at last published a book of poems, his 'Libro de Poemas.' There was to be a reading, and quite a large crowd attended. In the gathered circle as well as Emilio and Luis Bunuel there was a poet called Emilio Prados who was a friend of Rafael Alberti and together they brought a newcomer with them.

Alberti introduced him. "This guy is Salvador Domingo Felipe Jacinto Dali. He is an artist, a painter from Catalunia and he declares he is famous over there."

Dali stood up and said in all seriousness "That is correct." He caused some amusement because of his attire. Below a jacket of red stripes he wore britches and black silk stockings.

"My fame," declared Dali "is now spreading its wings like an expected bird, a harbinger of curiosity and doom that no gloved hand will stay. It is beyond doubt that I am descended in my ancestry from Moorish warriors."

Emilio Aladren called out "Thank you Senor Dali, you are welcome but bloody sit down, we wish to hear Federico who will read to us."

Federico stood and began to read. There was a music in his intonation almost like a song with pronounced rhythms and assonance as he told of girls gathering olives, of bullfighters, wives, orange trees, of Granada, of sorrow, of Sevilla, of cattlemen, of infidelity and a killing in the sierra and rivers of ice. His audience listened spellbound and silent. When he ended and sat down it was Dali who spoke again.

"It is a portent! You also make drawings of your words? I am amazed, we must discuss. I wish to shake your hand."

Federico went across to Dali, shook his hand and Dali said "It is necessary that you give me the book of your poems please."

Federico nodded and replied "If you wish. But I must tell you that my poems are made to be spoken aloud, not closed in a book all the time. A poet must laugh and weep with the people. His words, the yolk in the egg, are better tasted in a drama, a play or opera for all to hear."

"Very well Senor Opera, tomorrow we will sing together. Duet. I have, as you will discover, a famous voice!"

The students began to laugh, and then they decided that they would add their voices in song. As the petit soiree ended they marched, stamping, chanting and yelling, in a procession from the common room and to the corridors outside.

The lectures at the university ended for the summer break. Federico returned to Granada with de Falla. They decided to make a festival for the children of the farmers who had so little in their lives and no joy.

"I will write a play for them," said Federico, "And together, Manuel, we will make some music for the children to sing."

In due course the event was staged in the Lorca family home. His father made no objection, in fact, he was most agreeable. Sophie and I were asked along with Sanchez Carvagal and his wife and other friends including the Rosales. They had seen Federico's book of poems and commented that his ability to put words on paper was remarkable.

Crowding into the Rodriguez home the children were a sorry sight, a ragged, unruly, half-starved bunch of boys and girls who looked as if they had never once had a decent meal in their young lives. Federico asked his mother to arrange some food for them before they left. His brother Chico (Fancisco) worked the model puppet theatre which they had built some years ago, while Manuel played the piano and Federico played his guitarra, sang and did the different voices. There were several gypsy playlets, and Federico performed one of his own called 'The Girl who watered the Basil plant.' Afterwards, Dona Vicenta bade her *criadas* to bring each child a bowl of *caldo* (broth), slices of *jamon* and some almond cake.

When the children had feasted and made off for their homes we who remained were invited to stay for supper. After the laughter and yelling of the kids we were a sombre crowd. Dona Vicenta, a devout and faithful church-goer, observed that, following the death of Pope Benedict, a good man called Achille Ratti had accepted the mantle as Pius X1.

"He will be much needed," agreed Sanchez. "I do not care to mention this, but there are reports that Saldevik has been murdered. Zaragossa is now without its Archbishop."

There was a sense of shock followed by voices raised. Someone said the Ebro would again flow with the blood of saints. Don Rodriguez agreed. "This malaise spreads. Look what happened little more than one year ago". Heads nodded. There seemed to be no end to killing. In the colonies, in troubled Morocco, a force of 2,000 half-trained recruits in the Mellila Garrison had been slaughtered by Abdel Krim's tribal warriors. The proud General Silvestre, well regarded by King Alfonso, had cut his throat. Don Rodriguez remarked that some of the gitanos, so well-loved by his poetical son might have been involved in the affair, but Federico said it would not be so. Manuel agreed. He volunteered that whosoever was the cause of the disaster it would not help the cause of the King who might have made a bad choice of Commander-in-Chief.

Both Federico and Manuel were uneasy. They did not wish to discuss politics in this company. It would lead to arguments, for while they favoured the political Left, others, like the Rosales, were more conservative and strong monarchists. The subject was clearly giving pain. Dona Vicenta, too, was worried for her guests. "We hope and pray the situation will soon settle down, there is too much violence. Come, Federico, and you Senor de Falla, please honour us with more music. I am sure you have songs that were not for the children. We should like to hear them." I said Sophia and I would also like to hear them.

The two friends happily agreed, and the candles that were lit, accompanied by good wine, burned well into the night as an attentive audience listened to wedding songs, lullabies, love songs, ballads and chants some of which Federico had composed, and others that he had learned from labourers in the fields.

❋❋❋

Back at the Residencia it was generally accepted that Federico and Emilio Aladren, who was studying to be a sculptor, were the closest of friends as were Luis Bunuel and Dali. When they were not busy with their studies the four of them spent much of their free time together. Manuel de Falla was a gentle soul and something of a loner. It was Dali who, when not at the Academia de San Fernando, tended to initiate diversions.

"My muse, on the telefono," he declared nonsensically one evening, "has given the assurance that you are seekers of fame as I am already! Now, Emilio, and Federico my little *paloma* (dove), you are instructed to join me in my room and we will make some drawings. We can even paint if you wish, I have colours."

Emilio and Federico looked at each other with some unease. Unknown to the others they had already made some drawings together in the room they shared. Emilio, tired of making detailed representations of busts and torsos in the *museo*, had decided to use Federico as a model and had him remove his clothes. "It is always helpful to make a sketch before deciding to work in three dimensional form."

Federico for his part returned the compliment and persuaded Emilio to strip. He regarded his friend as handsome, as indeed he was, but he had not been prepared to find such a beautiful body before him. The smoothness, the grace and strength of his flesh shone like palest gold and touched his heart and every nerve in his body "Oh, Emelio! I must call you Apollo, you have captured the sun!" And he knew he longed to capture Emilio for himself alone, for he was more beautiful than the gypsy Juan, and even his hero the torero Mejias.

As the days and weeks and months passed the four students counted their blessings, for as well as developing their individual talents they learned more about each other. Friendships blossomed. Federico wrote more songs and ballads. He put aside his disappointment at the failure of his 'Butterfly' play, and told Emilio he was considering trying again. The political unrest and the agony that now darkened the entire country led him in a new direction.

"This time my play will tell a story many will understand. I will sing the praises of Mariana of Granada. You remember? She was in open opposition to King Ferdinand, and also in love with a lad known for his liberal sympathies. It destroys her. She faces execution with great courage."

"Ah Federico, you are playing safely to please the audience?"

"Emilio that is unkind. I write only what my heart tells me."

For his belief in himself, and the courage to make a second attempt to write a drama in verse he was amply rewarded. In June 1927 'Mariana Pineda' had its first night at the Teatro Goya in Barcelona. It was a pronounced success, a triumph that was repeated four months later at the Teatro Fontalba in Madrid. From the puppet plays of his early years Federico was becoming a mature playwright, applauded and admired. At the same time he was giving readings and lectures and contributing poems to literary magazines. There were celebrations in the Residencia, and in Granada the bohemian afficionados of the Alcala raised their glasses to their 'Remarkable Rico!' Not all, however was unbridled joy. Bunuel and Dali gave a party for him which was attended by their circle of friends. Only one was missing. It was Emilio. He was nowhere to be seen. In due course the reason became clear. Unbelievably he had found a new love, a girl studying at the Academy of Fine Art. In Federico's absence during rehearsals and first nights Emilio had checked out of the Residencia without a word. He did not even leave a note for his closest friend.

Federico froze. He fell into the deepest depression. He had lost the person he loved above all and could not come to terms with his loss. He refrained from writing. He cancelled a talk he had promised to give in Granada on Imagination and the role of the Poet as Dramatist. He said his role was ended. He sought Mejias whom he admired so much only to learn that he was on tour performing in bullrings to the north.

Bunuel and Dali attempted to console him. "Come my little dove," said Dali, "Open your wings and fly to me I am your doctor to make you well again. I hear you have been making some drawings, so bring your crayons to me. We will escape to my home and there together we will discover all new delights that charm the soul. Deliver up your heart to my therapeutic inspection!"

Federico was not impressed. The madness of Dali could not shift the dark cloud that enveloped him, but he agreed to accompany him for a brief visit to his family home at Cadaques in the far north east, a lonely outpost of society where the lower slopes of the Pyrenees fall into the sea. Bunuel equally was not impressed by Dali's flight north. He was now studying film production and had invited Dali's help. "Do not disappear for too long, this is not a holiday, my friend. I need you. We have work".

"Continue!" replied Dali. "I will return. Lay your eggs in your little nest and we will hatch them later. Have no fear, I am dreaming of the Academia and longing for your kisses!"

Having invited Federico to Cadaques and offered him accommodation in his comfortable family home, Dali encouraged the poet to exercise his skill as a draughtsman. It was early autumn when a hazy, golden light suffused the village the cliffs and beaches. Dali left him to explore on his own. Federico had said he wished to record some buildings that intrigued him. They were unlike those in Andalusia. On the first Sunday of his visit he perched on a wall facing the high white tower of Santa Maria which stood like a guardian angel above the crowded houses below. It was there he met Ana Maria, Dali's sister whom he had seen the previous evening at the supper table but had not spoken to her. However, she, on discovering him making his drawing, clearly wished to speak with him.

"Aha! The poet is discovered! And he is also a painter? May I look?"

Federico shook his head. "No, it is just a scribble. But that is a fine building."

"My family's church for many years." She peered closer and noted that Federico's sharp lines looked like a geometrical pattern. "Hm! Interesting! But not as good as my brother. Have you been inside Santa Maria? It is very beautiful!"

Ana remained at his side until he had completed his drawing. She studied him closely, sensing his isolation, and the air of sadness he could not conceal. By nature Ana was outspoken. "My brother is concerned for you, he tells me you have lost a friend. It was an accident?"

Federico did not reply. He liked the girl, but there were things you did not discuss and would never disclose. Least of all to one of the opposite sex whom you hardly knew. It was unlike him to be so withdrawn, and in fact, over the following few days, against his best intention, he dropped his guard. Ana had clearly taken a liking to him. Unexpectedly, he warmed to her. Dali said nothing. Indeed, much of the time he was absent. Federico assumed he was busy somewhere with canvas and easel, but Ana said it was not so. She wanted to confide. Caution was not her style.

"You must not say I told you, but my brother is several different people all wrapped up in one person. He is like a magician. His energy overcomes him. He becomes wild in his imagination, and is always restless as you may know. Now he has found a new friend. She is from a Russian family. My father is not pleased and worse still the girl is married! Perhaps you felt the difficulty in my home?" She paused then added "It is surprising because we thought my brother was, well I mean you can understand. His affections have always been for men. You must know this?"

Federico was stunned. She had clicked the latch and opened a Jack-in-the-Box. It was Ana who was the magician. She had worked a trick. She had guessed his true orientation from their first meeting. It was as if lines written in a foreign tongue had been translated and immediately made clear and simple. After the initial shock Federico experienced a sense of relief. Weeks of pain eased. Inextricably, the mists in his mind lifted like the mists that steamed up from the steep cliffs at the coast. His better self, his perception and humour began to return and his liking for Ana deepened. He saw her as he had seen Mariana, the heroine in his play, and felt he would like to read a little of it to her. A day or two later when he asked if she would like him to do so she eagerly responded.

"Please, Federico, of course! The newspaper report said the play was well received. I would like to have seen it. Barcelona is not so far, but you know a single lady cannot go alone."

Thus it was that, in the Dali house of Pubol, in the large salon with its plush furniture and wide windows, Federico gave a reading of Mariana Pineda to a compassionate and perceptive audience of one. He spoke and played every part. Ana was dazzled and delighted. As she listened she understood what her brother had once said of Federico when he first heard him reading. How beautifully he spoke and sang his ballads, his songs and lullabies. There was a constant vision of gypsies riding through olive groves with their silver leaves and beside flowing streams where the blue iris coloured the air. Dali once declared he had never known such extravagant passion, its flesh and bone quivering with a thousand flames of darkness, wild and beyond quenching.

Federico ended as the night rose up to touch the windows with stars and the poet and his listener fell silent. The aura of magic like a spell ebbed away, and Ana felt that air of melancholy she had sensed in him before. It wrapped itself in loneliness and for a while she saw him strangely removed like a shadow that slipped away to another place before he returned to her. But, their friendship flowered, and Federico agreed to stay in Cadaques for a few days longer than planned. Dali was pleased that the two of them had grown so close.

By day Federico and Ana took long walks together on the steep cliffs of Creus and down on the shingle beaches. Dali declared the world had now found peace and celebrated by purchasing a canary in a cage to sing for him during the day. He then caught cicadas which, he announced, would sing him to sleep at night. And that was not all. The night before Federico was to take his leave, a farewell party on the beach was arranged. Better than the gannets and gulls that made the cliffs their home Dali loved his cache of swans that swam in a small, sheltered bay. That night a full moon cast the shadows of the party-goers on the rocks and the red cliffs that Dali so often chose to paint. Servants from the big house lit a fire, then roasted a suckling pig, and brought wine. So they ate and danced and villagers came to join them. Dali stripped and, naked, jumped into the water. He had tied lighted candles to the necks of several swans and together they swam to and fro like a glitter of stars. Someone brought a guitarra for Federico and he sang an impromptu song — "How sharp is the edge of moon, moon, to tear ribbons of white waves in the sky!"

The following morning, with a sore head, he said his goodbyes and promised Ana that they would surely meet again. Then he turned his face to the south, to Barcelona, and across country to Madrid and the Residencia.

Part Three

The Poet Of The People

When Dona Vicenta called to see me she did not bring good news.

"Federico came home for a short visit and had many arguments with his father. He announced that he is a poet, that he was born as a poet just as other people are born blind or lame. Perhaps you can understand, as I do very well. My husband is saying he will no longer pay for Federico at the Residencia and this is unfair. Federico has written to us from Madrid and I know he studies very hard."

I was not surprised to hear this, but I was disappointed that Don Rodriguez would no longer support his son.

"Senor Castejou, I feel I may ask a favour, for you have always been a friend of my son. It would be a good help if you could speak to my husband."

Much as I regarded Dona Vicenta with affection I did not relish a meeting with Don Rodriguez to discuss Federico's future. If there was a problem it was for the family to find a solution, and while I was sympathetic, it was not for me to say.

Dona Vicenta continued "You see, Federico has always been my favourite child, and I feel his pain. I can remember so well when he was very young he used to play with the other farmers' children on the *Vega*. He was unhappy because they had nothing and he had so much here in my home. He always tried to help the *campesinos*. That is his nature."

A problem shared does not mean a problem solved, but I thought to discuss the situation with Sophia. She understood Federico as well as anyone and regarded him with a mixture of awe and great affection.

"You should not think twice," was her response. "You of all people should understand. We know Federico is very different from other young men of intelligence. He is remarkable. He possesses a magic, an aura difficult to define and he seems to have a fire burning in him. He has a wonderful gift. You know this as well as I know it. I think it is important that he is allowed to continue his studies at the Residencia. Also, you know as well as I that he meets with many and varied talents there, and this must surely help his work."

Sophia was, of course, perfectly correct. So I told Dona Vicenta that I would agree to speak with her husband. But I added that I did not think it would be of great help.

I was surprised and relieved when he received me kindly. "I know why you have come," he said. "My wife has been talking to you. Please sit down."

In my mind I had decided upon a plan. It was simple. I reminded Don Rodriguez that Federico not only possessed a remarkable and genuine gift, but he was receiving an education that most families could never afford for their children.

"Consider, sir, what he is really doing," I said. "He is associating with people of intelligence and maturity who have many talents. They are musicians and writers, and come not only from our country but from France, from England, even Germany. From all that I hear, they are a noisy, very vocal group but they appear to be finding new ways forward for artistic creation which reflects well on our country."

Don Rodriguez was not impressed. Did he understand what I was trying to say? I continued. "His verses and indeed all his writings, as you must know, are very well received. The new play has proved a success. But more than this, he is giving lectures on his work and the work of others and I think this can make our country very proud."

"I doubt it," Rodriguez replied. "Our country has no time for this. There is great disturbance. Much violence. Plays and music may be accepted in a time of peace, but our country's most urgent duty now is to deal with the anarchists, and others who are causing such trouble. I do not see that poetry has any use for us at this time."

"With respect, sir, I believe that it has, and it is important."

If this was to be a debate I began to wish I had the help of the good Professor Aragon. I could not work miracles, but perhaps he might.

"All I suggest is that you give your son more time. He surely deserves his success. I believe he can only bring credit to your family, and to Granada as well."

My words appeared to give him pause. He was not antagonistic and I think he realised I was trying to help matters. But, had I won my case? Something told me progress was made. Before I left he was good enough to shake my hand. That could mean anything. But, he also offered me a cigar.

"The very best," he said with half a smile. "From Havana."

❈❈❈

A schoolmaster should not become involved in politics, and my intention was always to keep a balanced and moderate view. If anyone asked Sophia and I about our inclinations we would answer Liberal. Even so I could not help but have some sympathy with the farmer Rodriguez. Apart from his concern with Federico there was no doubt he must have other problems. Throughout the country, and particularly in Andalusia, the workers on the land are causing riots, demanding a fairer deal from the land owners. It is so bad the Guardia Civil are being called in time after time. The workers' patience is at breaking point, and they are becoming increasingly violent. Many are being arrested, no one escapes and merciless killings are being reported.

I had never expected my friend Sanchez Carvajal to suffer depression, but even this busy and honest man had a dark brow when we met. "We now have a big problem," he complained. "The Cortes is becoming a ship with no rudder. There is no Government, unless you call Primo, that laughable *comico* (comedian) a government. And I do not!"

He was referring to Miguel Primo de Rivera, the Captain General from the province of Catalunia who had won the confidence of King Alfonso. I said that from what I had read in Sanchez's own newspaper Primo seemed to be an affable, charismatic man who was popular, and not least with the ladies.

"Yes, Luis. So it seems. He may be a big bull of a man, but he has no political sense."

"Well, you may say that, but he has declared himself to be the saviour of our country. It is clear that he has the support of the Army, many Generals, also the Church and people in industry as well."

"That may be. Sure, he is guarding Alfonso's position but, do not forget, he has now openly appointed himself dictator and declared that we are in a state of war. He is giving himself the right to control all things, even Bankers, the universities, engineering companies, the miners, and he cannot do it! He has not the ability. Take my word, he is only Army, he cannot understand civil affairs. He will not last long. The country will not have it. Would you trust yet another dictator?"

I realised that, more and more, it was a question of wait and see. I said "We who are teachers, civil servants district councillors can do nothing. To be in opposition to government, any government, is as good as accepting a visiting card to suicide. Maybe it is the same for journalists as well?"

The good Sanchez did not laugh. Just a wan smile. "I think," he said, "it is again time for a glass of my good brandy. Shall we?"

I did not refuse. And, I confess, I was a little late getting home that evening.

As the months passed the doubts that Sanchez had voiced became only too real. The optimism with which Primo de Rivera brought to his dictatorship to save the nation started to dissolve. He was no longer 'the iron man'. His military solution simply did not succeed. The peseta was devalued, unemployment rose and the standard of living declined steeply. There were more strikes and demonstrations as the farm workers rose against him. The popularity he had enjoyed earlier evaporated and left him in despair. In January (1930) he resigned and fled to Paris where, it is reported, he died of a broken heart. Some time later, Sanchez, adding to his prophesy, said: "It is inevitable. A national disaster. The King himself championed Primo and I cannot see that even he will remain much longer, he has little or no support."

He was proved right again. The Church could not save Alfonso and he, too, has now gone into exile. It is said that Don Miguel Maura will attempt to establish a provisional government.

✳✳✳

It is a pleasure for me now to record that over the past few months events have improved in certain quarters. I do not of course mean on the political stage. I mean there has been a good development for Federico. Don Rodriquez has relented and agreed to pay the fees for the Residencia. This I believe was mainly due to the influence of Dona Vicenta who was in regular correspondence with her son and in a position to provide reassurance as to the value of his time in Madrid. For his part, as his mother told me, Federico continued to write to her.

'I have to tell you the Residencia will change the world, not just my world but the lives of many, and perhaps even of countries. It is a powerhouse for

change, for an outlook that is new. We cannot fail. Old values are slipping away in spite of the two-faced politicians, greedy lawyers and bastard men of war with impossible ambitions. And who is making this change? It is good friends of mine right here. Rafael (Alberti), Luis (Bunuel), darling Dali, and me, and many others including the visitors who come to us. They come to see the Residencia, to praise. lecture and encourage us. I work and study and read very hard and am inspired. With my friends I defend Art. True Art. It is in all my work.'

Dona Vicenta sometimes expressed her concern to me that her son was spending too much time with his friends. "I tell him to keep his head down on his books. He says he has completed the gypsy ballads he calls Romancero Gitano, and requires to get them. published. I think I am becoming his agent and must appeal for funds to my husband. You can understand Luis that sometimes I feel it would be better not to have a son who is a poet!"

I am sure she did not really mean that. Had she forgotten his book of gypsy ballads? It had become a remarkable success and now is, despite the turbulent times, greatly admired throughout the country. Cynics and critics alike are sitting up and taking notice. Federico is becoming well known and is being called 'the Gypsy Poet.' He says he does not like this title. It does not please him. He prefers to be called the poet of the people, the cattlemen and the peasants, and he again asserts that his poems came from the soil, the roots of his land and especially from Granada, Cordoba and Sevilla, the Andalusia he loves. His energy seems to me to be amazing, for as well as his poems and songs he has been working on a play called The Shoemakers Wonderful Wife, he has edited and contributed to a literary magazine and has been giving lectures to fellow students in the Residencia and also here in public on his visits home.

※※※

Standing before a group of new students at the Residencia Federico announced that on this occasion he would not give a talk about his own work. That would come later. "I prefer today," he said "to consider the visual arts and to examine the work of my good friend

Salvador Dali who is frequently with us here, always ready to delight us in his own eccentric manner." He paused. "Perhaps I should not use the word eccentric. That is for cynics and philistines. I would rather characterise his work as rising from the deep unconscious. His imagination is remarkable and the volume of his work so far is of very first importance. I know this because I am close to him and in many ways my work echoes his imagination just as his often reflects mine.

In saying this we cannot be considered to be artistic twins. For while much of my inspiration arises from my very close association with the ordinary people of the land, Dali's is bred in an altogether different zone. You may say that we both live our dreams, but Salvador's inspiration is not of this world. He comes from his own realm of 'another place.' For him reason and any sense of rationality whatsoever is suspended. Our motives are similar, but our beginnings are very different. Where you were born, and what you allowed yourself to absorb from the Past is what enables you to become what and who you are.

"Salvador reaches deeply beyond what you may call reality. He himself declares that he suspends reason and even describes his work as 'critical paranoia.' He will for example paint a range of hills that look like a dog. Or he will paint a man with an apple for a face. Historians in future will no doubt lead you down the path to where they say his inspiration began. For my part I firmly believe it does not arise from dwelling on acknowledged classical painters, but from 'literature', from the writings of Baudelaire and Rimbaud, also Eduard and Cocteau. Thus it is the work of poets, not of painters that in the first instance set Salvador on the path he follows today."

The students listened attentively as Federico continued to inform their imagination. He encouraged them to look at Dali's work discarding their pre-conceived ideas of what art should be. He advised them to be equally prepared to note that beneath Dali's images, his technique and skill revealed a true master of his craft, confident and at ease with his own genius, exhibiting brilliant linear ability as well as a joyous celebration of colour. It was hoped by many of the students that Dali himself would, in return, pay tribute publicly to Federico. He did not do so, but privately, in a letter, he described his first reaction to his personality, his aura which he found overwhelming. As for the poetry it was blood red, sublime, quivering with a thousand fires of unquenchable flames.

While many of Federico's poems blaze with the magic of words 'married' one to another in a manner that can be understood, many a time they present a contrapuntal edge which may surprise the listener like the sounding of a cracked bell, or the heaven-sent harmony of a suite of music by Debussy. He dedicates poems to friends but does not write to please a given audience. His images in their twists and turns erupt from his deepest self. He is all too conscious that he does not succeed every time he puts pen to paper, and the more work flows from his mouth the more he becomes self-critical. He writes and re-writes constantly. Seldom is there any humour in his ballads and songs as again and again they tell of love never found, of longing, of meeting and leaving, of loss, anguish, isolation and sorrow. Above all he is confronted by the Shadow, the constant presence of what he calls "the heartless anonymity of Death." By contrast joy, admiration and respect do appear in many poems and it is not only the landscape and sheer beauty of Andalusia, the olive groves, the rivers, the poplars and pines and the gardens of flowers that haunt him, it is also the landscape of the heart and "the river of the mind that knows no horizon." Simply put his poems and songs touch something beyond human life.

Unhappily, not all was as serene, or simple as it sounds. I recorded in my journal that Federico began to quarrel with his publishers. There were disagreements and he became depressed. He wrote to his mother that he had stumbled upon a deep ravine, a cavern in his dreams from which he could not climb, a place eternally dark and where he longed to find daylight but was prevented. His depression deepened. Even love tasted sour. The family became seriously concerned. Dona Vicenta wrote to me *'It is not beyond possibility that Federico's frustration and unhappiness could reach a point of no return, and knowing him as I do this could lead to disaster. He has often expressed a wish to learn to speak English. We see no harm in this and have now suggested to him that he might care to visit the new world. America. We feel the change of landscape and culture might help. I have asked Professor Aragon to speak with him. Perhaps a new world could work a little miracle?'*

On my occasional meetings with Dona Vicenta I usually came away with the feeling that in spite of the darkening political landscape, not all was lost for Granada or even Andalusia itself. But on the last occasion that we talked she said in no uncertain terms that her husband had become increasingly uneasy. "The reign, as he puts it, of Primo de Rivera had broken apart. He had every opportunity to take action and improve the situation for the farmers. All farmers, But he did nothing, Since then we have a new cabal of politicos and only God knows what will happen to us."

The situation was certainly confused with many other politicians threatening to leave the political stage in Madrid. As I considered this it was ironic that I should hear that Federico was also leaving Madrid and was on his way to America. His association with the Residencia had won him a place at Columbia University, New York where he would study English.

✸✸✸

From all that I hear his long journey to 'The New World' did not live up to expectations. At the outset he was pleased, having been met off the boat by several friends who greeted him warmly, and took him to his living quarters in a hall of residence at the university. During the following days and weeks instead of concentrating on his intended attempt to learn English through a course in English Language and Literature, he neglected his studies, preferring to see as much as possible of the great city. He was taken to the New York Stock Exchange which he hated, and to Harlem which he loved. He was feted, much admired, and went to parties where, beating prohibition, he drank gin and entertained friends and admirers alike with his songs at the piano. He was deeply affected by the blatant materialism of the culture he encountered and was angered by the manner in which the coloured population, the Negroes, were treated. As time passed his pleasure and enthusiasms faded and loneliness overtook him. His unhappiness was tempered by a visit during the August vacation to his English friend Philip Cummings who had a log cabin holiday home on the shores of Lake Eden in Vermont. In letters to his family it became clear that his visit to the new world was not so much an adventure as a sad pilgrimage.

'The buildings in the centre of the city, as I expected, have been built very high, but I see no beauty in them. They are the decaying teeth of a dying giant. I tremble to think of skyscrapers, and how to work or live in them. Here, the world turns too rapidly, with the citizens striving to catch up, but catch up to what? If their aim is, as I suspect, the accumulation of wealth, then they will be disappointed. Newspapers shout alarming headlines. SHARE PRICES COLLAPSE. Last week on the market losses amounted to $30 billion. Brokers are going bankrupt. Street corners show unemployment as thousands lose their work, and many lose their homes. People say a depression is on its way, but I say it has arrived.'

To de Falla he wrote: *'You may wish to come here soon, but I do not advise it. So far the only music I have found was in the Roseland Ballroom. A band called Fletcher Henderson was playing jazz with Louis Armstrong. But it was only for white people, the blacks were not allowed in. It was the same at the Sunset Café. I tell you, Manuel, the sun is setting on this city. Johnny black man is a slave condemned to sweep the gutter, to serve his white master at table, to clean his shoes in the street. And for the population no liquor is allowed. Those who want alcohol have to go to private clubs they call speakeasies where there are drugs. It is said there are 100,000 of them between the city and Canada. Those who own them are criminals breaking the law.'*

Federico also wrote to his Professor, Jorge Aragon: *'I did not expect to long for my Granada. I surprise myself. But here I feel very far away, even from myself and I find no comfort in the University. It is a fine place but I cannot speak with the students, nor do they seek to speak to me. As for study, you know I have already found great interest in Shakespeare and in Chekhov, so there is little more to find here except the poetry of T. S. Eliot. I have read the Waste Land. It is a magnificent work. But the English language is not as easy as I had thought. I read but cannot pronounce it. I prefer to do my own work and am busy with one long play, a shorter one, and poems.'*

To my surprise I also received a letter: *'I think you would be interested in my college, it is in Morningside Heights, Manhattan. The library has millions of books, but I am stopping my course. I have a new friend, Paco, he is from Mexico and lives in Harlem, the place for Afro-Americans, also Jewish people and many Puerto Ricans who work in the clothing business. It has been so hot in the city, very humid, I went out to Vermont for the rest of Summer, a place called Eden Mills. It is not the garden of Eden, and not like our Generalife, but there was sweet air, fine hills and the trees beginning to weep blood. Back in the city I also weep. There is a very large Catholic presence, but these Christians do nothing to care for the poor. There are beggars on the streets. Why will they not give some help?'*

I felt worried for him. His visit to America was proving to be a mistake. But it was Dona Vicenta who said I should not be too concerned. She had received some delightful letters. He had gone over to Cuba and found the people there more friendly and interested in his poetry. "He could not work well in New York, he said he was unhappy, but he liked Cuba and was inspired."

I learned later that he gave two lectures, one of them on the theory and function of the duende. His audience consisted of Friends of The Arts Club of Havana. It was large and very mixed. Many of the young people, eager to see and hear the poet they regarded as one of their own, had come from Catalunia, Andalusia, and Galicia. There were also descendants of immigrants from Portugal, Italy, and even Russia. All seemed eager to listen and try to understand what he meant when speaking of the duende. He addressed the gathering boldly, naturally with, as was his custom, papers in hand bearing the words he had carefully crafted. He rarely if ever spoke without his papers. The duende, he said, was easily recognised by the gitanos and by poets, artists and musicians everywhere, people, he reminded them, like his good friend de Falla with whom he had worked closely on flamenco and the puppet plays of his youth. Duende was 'dark sounds.' A mystery that was widely recognised but which few rarely understood. It concerned the act of creativity and culture but was not the act itself, rather was it that dark area that lay beneath, that knew neither Age nor Time. It was a power given to, or inherited by the performer concerned who had an inborn intimation of excellence, of perfection in their individual, chosen art. They knew the peak of true emotion was only found if there was duende. Cervantes had duende, as did many of the Andalusian flamenco singers and dancers. He cited the example of the torero in the corrida. Not every one of them had duende, but those who performed brilliantly with the bull, facing, fighting and accepting the possibility or the inevitability of death, yes, they had duende.

Federico's lecture continued for a further hour and among other things magically ushered in words about angels, of ballads and poems, and there were classical references which came as no surprise to those who knew his work. On this occasion, as he spoke his audience was captured and enchanted. At the end he was greeted with waves of applause. Many in the audience struggled to get near him, to touch him, to shake his hand.

As well as giving a second lecture, in letters home it seems that Federico found time to add the finishing touches to his play The Shoemakers Wonderful Wife, and to complete a number of poems, ballads and sonnets. Many were dedicated to friends and people he loved or admired and which he had started before returning to Madrid where, in due time, they were published. I recall one of his early ones. It was called 'Sonnet in tribute to Manuel de Falla, offering him flowers.'

> 'Warm lyre of glowing silver
> of firm accent and supple nerve
> with your hands of love you have drawn
> voices and foliage of passionate Spain.

In our own blood is the fountain
from which your reason and dreams have sprung.
Clean Algebra of serene brow
Discipline and passion for what is dreamed.

Eight provinces of Andalusia
olive tree in the breeze, oars on the sea,
they sing, Manuel de Falla, your joy.

With the laurel and these flowers we bring .
friends of your home. On this day
we offer you pure, simple friendship.'

His poems also included an Ode to Walt Whitman, whom he admired, and a crushing condemnation of New York, a city in which he could find nothing to admire and that offered no inspiration. Much of the work he attempted carried the tilt and dizziness of surrealism but it did not disguise his anger at the treatment of the Negroes. His heartfelt sorrow also revealed his warmth towards them. 'There is no anguish that compares with your oppression or with the shudder of your blood in the dark eclipse, or with garnet violence deaf and dumb in the dusk.'

❈❈❈

It was my good wife Sophia who gave me the news. "Dona Vicenta wished to see you but you were still at the school. She said one of Federico's plays has been shown at the Teatro Espanol in Madrid and it is a great success for him!"

"That will be The Shoemaker's Wonderful Wife," I replied. "I heard he had been working on it. The family will be very pleased. I also. And I have some good news. At last the Government is to increase the number of teachers throughout the land, and those who are now older like me are to have an increase in pay!"

Sophia did not disguise her pleasure. She curtsied. "Very good, sir! Then I shall give you a kiss! It is what you deserve, you work very hard for your school."

The success of Federico's play was widely acknowledged, not simply in Madrid but throughout the country and in France and Italy as well. Despite the political situation, education and cultural affairs oddly and surprisingly began to shine as never before. It was generally acknowledged, however, that the agrarian malaise continued. I was reminded of this by Sanchez. His newspapers' reports made dismal reading as the political turmoil continued. Alcala Zamora, the President of the Government resigned, and with him went Maura who had become Minister of the Interior. In the following election the Republicans won a mandate to rule and Azana took over as Prime Minister.

"A change for the better, perhaps," said Sanchez. "And that was good news about Federico. But he will know as well as I do that the majority of our farm workers today are still illiterate. The new Government may try to help but the fact is we are still a peasant economy and even here in Andalusia many families are near to starvation. Political promises are nothing but hot air. No subsidies. No action. It is a disgrace."

I had to agree, but a month or so later Federico's family surprised me with brighter news. They declared, and with a justifiable note of pride, that Federico was returning to Granada on what Dona Vicenta called "a special mission." He had contacted our cities' mayor, with a request that he be allowed to take a group of actors to the poorer parts of the country where they would perform plays and poetry to encourage the campesinios learning and understanding. In "an educational reconnaissance" he would visit the pueblos and to this end he would require financial aid. The mayor was in full agreement, but had to approach the Government for money to fund the project. The timing was accidental, but fortunate. The new government was Republican and responded favourably to the mayor of Granada's request. Funding, was duly agreed and Federico wasted no time in bringing together a troupe of young students from Madrid. He formed a company he called La Barraca and, as producer, director and actor planned his tour to perform primarily for rural audiences.

Dona Vicenta told me: "We had good discussions on what plays Federico would choose. It was decided there should be some classical drama perhaps from Lope de Vega and Calderon, with some of his own work, including songs and ballads. He has a new puppet play called Don Cristobal and is determined to devise his own style of performance. It is a great opportunity and I think he has never been so happy." She added with a wink: "I think, mister schoolmaster, your student and my child will be famous!"

I replied that I, too, was optimistic for Federico's future, but when Sophia and I were discussing it at home she said she was not so sure. "I know he is brilliant but it is a labour for him, as if he carries a load on his back which is too heavy."

"Why do you say that? I think he is happier now than before, the family believes it is so. He is producing so many fine poems, and, I am told he is working on some new plays."

"Luis, you know what I mean. It is his personal life. No one will speak of it, but I am sure. I can tell, and I am sorry for him."

It had not occurred to me that Sophia could be so perceptive. I had never spoken of Federico's association with his male friends, and I would not think of him in this way. After all, women also seemed to be very attracted to him. I did not wish to continue this conversation but said "Federico is a poet, he has friends who are poets and artists and musicians. and many, especially in theatre and drama, are like him."

"Well, that is very sad."

I answered that we would not speak of it, and I too was sad. I loved my Sophia and did not care to argue with her. Especially when, I had to admit, her opinions were often correct and she would not change her mind!

✳✳✳

For nine months all through the hot summer La Barraca's progress was followed with wide interest and there was much talk of which villages the touring company would visit. In fact, they travelled to many pueblos, large and small, performing in halls and when the halls were not available, or too small, the company played under the evening sun in squares and gardens. The places ranged from nearby Antequera, Osuna on the road to Sevilla, to Andujar beyond Cordoba and as far as Terrega beyond Lerida and to La Puebla de Hijar near Zaragoza. The *campesinos* with their families turned out and greeted the itinerant group of players with surprising enthusiasm.

In a letter to his mother Federica also expressed surprise. He wrote *"After Don Cristobal, which we played on a proper stage, they shouted for me to come forward. Mothers with their children wanted to shake my hand, and for one hour they stood in a line. They came to me poor as they were, smiling and wanting to say thank you. I was moved to tears, they understood everything. Their bellies were empty but their hearts were full. I was grateful, but angry that they had so little."*

Back in Granada I felt that the family suffered for him. They knew, as I knew, that his concern for the great numbers of half-starved farm workers was genuine. I realised that, unhappily, it might create in him a deep sadness and frustration which could injure the sense of joy and success that he deserved.

Part Four

Critics Write Rave Notices

The dark night of an entire nation in conflict with itself seemed inevitable. A night with no moon, a nightmare offering no daybreak, no solution, no salvation. That is how it seemed to me, and Sanchez too was losing hope. It was his opinion that Cardinal Segura, the Archbishop of Toledo and Primate of Spain in condemning the Republican government had created mayhem. A point of no return.

"He should have held his tongue and exercised a little patience, he was too hasty and look what has ensued. An unholy war! He declared that Alfonso should return, and now see what a disaster he has created!"

It was obvious that republican sympathisers would retaliate, and they, too, lacked patience. There were riots and marches. Churches and convents were attacked and burned. Open declarations rang from cities to the poorest in the land. Hot heads called for religious teaching to be illegal, others called for divorce to be made legal and even cried for Easter to be banned. Increasing unemployment followed, especially in the south among young people. To say that there was dismay in Granada was a grotesque understatement. In the cafes, in once sedate and sensible homes, among the richer folk who lived in the Bib-Rambla, and the Plaza Campillo the strongest opinions were voiced leading to arguments that set families against each other. It was worse, far worse for the *campesinos*. It was estimated that many thousands of families were starving, yes, even from Toledo to Andalusia. Miners and building workers defied the government, and it was reported that in Casas Viejas near Cadiz some 21 *campesinos* were slaughtered giving rise to further violence. The poorer people everywhere demanded justice, calling for a fairer distribution of land. The FAI, an anarchist federation, was established and supported by the Federation of Land workers, but both failed, defeated by CEDA, the Catholics who were the largest party in the Cortes.

I said to Sophia, who was deeply troubled, that it was in times like this that one feared the worst and that the violence might spread to bring harm even to professors, teachers, civil servants and many others who served the community. But, the fact was there had never before been a time like this, at least for us. It was impossible to predict what might befall, but we could be thankful for one thing. Don Garcia Rodriguez, with Dona Vicenta and the family and servants had moved to Granada. It was a sensible move, as Dona Vicenta told me. "Many farm owners lost everything when the *campesinos* rebelled. My husband says the government bills on agrarian reform led to thousands of hectares of land being taken from landowners."

I asked Dona Vicenta if she had any news of Federico, and she replied that he was again up country with La Barraca. "I told him he should now stop the tour, it is too dangerous, but he takes no notice, and now of all things he is in Barcelona. That is not good."

I replied that, while it was wonderful that he could continue his work, it was even more remarkable that he could take poetic drama to a multitude of oppressed and half-starved peasants. In fact, his audience in Barcelona was sophisticated. For them he read from his recent work 'Poet in New York,' which reflected his period of surrealism. Later he also read to some of his friends his new play called 'Blood Wedding' and six months later it was staged at the Teatro Beatriz in Madrid. He knew he had created something entirely different to traditional drama but did not expect the acclaim with which it was greeted. The critics wrote rave notices and the public flocked to see the production. Among them was Professor Jorge Aragon who was now working at Madrid University. He wrote a letter of unbounded enthusiasm to me.

'I have to tell you Luis that in an audience I have never witnessed such scenes. It was as if a starving public had been given a veritable feast of delicious food they had never before tasted!'

I respected the professor's view. He was not usually given to such exaggeration. I felt the sad truth was that the 'veritable feast' of words did not fill empty stomachs. He continued *'I was permitted to witness a dress rehearsal of this play. I was amazed. The characters do not have personal names, they are simply called The Mothers, The Bride, The Servant and so on., only one character has a true name:- Leonardo. And let me describe the staging. Much of the setting is in a room painted yellow. The players are all dressed in black and at times they adopt still poses as in a tableaux. There is music and of course songs and poetry. I cannot really describe it, you must see the play for yourself. This is a tragedy based on a true happening when a bride who is about to be married runs away with a lover.'*

A true happening? It could be. In a flash my memory lit like a light being switched. on. I saw the faces of Sophia's friends around the table. Alicia's sister, of course. What I found more astonishing was the sheer volume of work that flowed from Federico. At the Teatro Espanol he staged his play 'The Love of Don Perlimplin' and with Manuel de Falla he produced 'Love the Magician' for the students at the Residencia. The Professor also reported that Federico was working on another play to be called 'Yerma.' Some months later he attended a performance of the play and mentioned it in a talk he gave to the students at the Residencia when lecturing on Lope de Vega, our classical poets and baroque drama.

"There is no doubt," he said " that Federico Garcia Lorca's grasp of the three-act dramatic form stems from his reading of at least some of Lope de Vega's work. He has, and always had from the beginning a large appetite for the work of other poets. He seems to swallow and digest the style and instinct of great masters and allows it to flavour his own unique ability when bringing his poetry like a living pulse to dramatic performance in the theatre.

"Lope de Vega was, as your studies will have informed you, a lyric poet in his own right with a genius for comedy. You will recall that he was a prolific author and lover. His amorous adventures led to his banishment from Castile for eight years during which time he continued to produce a mass of work. By the time of his death in 1635 he had written at least 1,500 plays, 3,000 sonnets, 9 epic poems, 3 novels and 4 novellas! An astonishing achievement when you consider that he served in the navy, sailed with the Armada against England and, later, became a priest while privately retaining the very personal services of Marta de Nevares, who was just one of his many lovers.

"The great difference between the nation's poet of the 17th century and Federico Lorca today is that the first wrote comedy while Lorca makes a haunting beauty out of sadness and tragedy. You might wish to compare and contrast Blood Wedding with, for example, a tragedy by Shakespeare."

Little did the good professor know, until later, that at the very time he was lecturing on Spanish literature Federico was writing an elegy on the death of his great friend, one of his true loves, the bullfighter Ignacio Sanchez Mejias who had been killed in the corrida. He called the poem a *Llanto*, a lament. It contained a repeated line that rang through the verses: 'At five in the afternoon.' It was like the tolling of a bell, repeated and repeated. There was blood in the sand as the torero was gored to death. The lines sang and sobbed, seeping like blood from an open wound, from the savagely hurt heart of the poet unable to contain his grief. Bells rang. Crowds gathered at street corners, silent. Waiting. The magnificent tolling of grief rang on and on, line after line until the final words. He wrote that not for a long time would there be an Andalusian who was so noble, and adventurous. Yes, his torero, his love was *valiente* (brave). The mystery and certainty of Death in Life was, he felt, of his own flesh and blood. Mejias's death in the ring stained his memory and would do so for years to come.

Among my colleagues and friends, and equally among cynical counsellors and ambitious lawyers and politicians, the blood of one graceful and popular torero was as nothing compared to the blood that seeped then flowed freely from the heart of my country. Everywhere wounds appeared. In a small *pueblo* called Castilblanco, it was reported that some local socialists wished to demonstrate against the governor of Badajoz. The Government refused to allow a demonstration however peaceful and sent the Guardia Civil to keep order on the streets. It proved to be a clumsy decision, for when the villagers attempted to hold a protest meeting and the Guardia Civil stepped in to prevent it they were set upon. Several were killed, others had their eyes gouged out and suffered multiple stab wounds and bodies were mutilated. There were similar riots and affrays in other pueblos. It came as no surprise, for how long had the peasants suffered?

The heart and centre of the country is now a virtual desert. Food is scarce. It is brought in from a few favoured valleys and the coast, but it is not sufficient. Most farms are very small, many producing only olives and wine and neglecting other crops. The struggling Government is attempting reform but the plan to give land workers a better deal has been resisted in the Cortes. In fact, the workers' pay of 3.50 pesetas per day has been doubled, but it makes little difference. Worse still, our entire country is now riding waves of anger as provincial councils seek self government with Catalunia and the Basque communities in the north making a bid for home rule and seeking control over justice, education and communications.

According to Sanchez in some towns schools are being closed as rioting and violence flares, bringing danger to whole communities. Granada is the exception, but I felt it was time that I should retire. It was a difficult decision because I am not rich and my savings are small. Sophia was worried. She did not think I should cease work.

"Luis, you love your teaching. I cannot believe you should retire. What will you do? It is a bad decision. And what will happen to us? You realise we cannot manage if we have only one *sueldo* (salary)."

I agreed it was a problem, but had a possible answer. We might manage if I could take some part-time work. "I will make an appointment to see the Council. Perhaps they might give me two days of work in the office, it would be enough."

Sophia replied that she had a better solution. "Why do you not speak with the Mayor? At least he could advise you. They say he is a good man."

As usual she was right. I admit it was sensible. I would have a word with him. He was very popular in Granada and much admired. I would do it. "My dear Sophia, what would I do without your brain!"

"You can give me a kiss. That is the price of my brain! When you are teaching there is never time for a kiss."

Luis, I said to myself, how can you be so lucky? It was worth more than one kiss, for when I spoke with the Mayor he agreed to help and offered me three half days of secretarial work to be paid as for two whole days. When I told Sophia she was happy and said "Now I will see more of my husband. I will teach you cooking!"

Part Five

Enter The Celebrity

As the days passed, with more time to myself, I felt a little lost. My routine was altered, but it did not suit me, for by nature I am not an idle person. I should have used my imagination. Writing a journal is all very well, and I will continue to record some political observations. But also I felt a sense of guilt because writing can be a solitary and selfish activity. I considered returning to the university and perhaps studying Art history or even attempting a course in painting. But I soon discarded this idea, for I am not good with pencil or brush.

When December came there was more news of Federico's continuing success. I was not surprised but my friend Sanchez was expressing some doubts as we sat over our drinks at the Alcala.

"It is remarkable that Lorca can continue his work. His world, and yours and mine Luis, is changing fast and there is confusion. Look at Azana, his support in the Cortes appears to be weakening. He is up against so many different factions."

I knew what he meant. The Catholic Church was showing more muscle, Fascist ideology was gaining ground while, at the same time it was reported that a new Falangist group had raised its head close to us here in Andalusia.

"It is a political pudding," observed Sanchez. "There are too many conflicting ingredients that can never mix. I hear our university students are finding a new voice and they are demonstrating against Marxism and the communists who, in turn, are erecting barriers against those Fascists. It is madness, a poisoned pudding, and in the meantime we are forgetting a most important change on the home front. Women are to have the vote!"

I said "And why not? That can surely be a change for the better. You know Sanchez, I am beginning to think you should get into politics. Go and stir that pudding. You can fight for justice and equality!"

"Personally, you know that is not on my table. As a journalist I cannot be to the Left or to the Right. I am pig in the middle. It is you who should be in politics, now you have the time. Be in the fashion, Luis! What would be your Party?"

"Like Federico I would seek a fairer world for the land workers, the *campesinos*."

"That is good thinking but it will not happen. You know that we have never had a balanced economy. There are too many generals in the Army, too many vocal priests in the Church, and too many landowners attempting to emulate the rich industrial bosses in the North."

That evening, when I told Sophia of my conversation with Sanchez she pulled a face and exclaimed "You men! What a waste of time you spend in idle discussions, you are worse than my friends with their families, yes, they gossip also but at least they are practical. They have to be."

I promised I would be practical tonight and help with the dishes. As I did so Sophia said "The talk is all of Federico. You have heard the news?"

I had heard some of it. At second hand. Later, the facts became clear from letters he wrote. The most exciting fact was that Federico had been invited to take one of his plays to Argentina. It turned out that he would take more than Blood Wedding, He was encouraged by the Arts Club, the university, writers, admirers, actors, and. theatrical impressarios in Buenos Aires who knew of his work and were eager to meet him. Thus it was that he boarded a transatlantic liner at Barcelona and took the long journey West, calling at Las Palmas, Rio de Janeiro, and Montevideo before reaching Buenos Aires. It was a long journey, but Federico used his time to good effect, working on poems and a new play as well as Mariana Pineda, Blood Wedding and The Shoemaker's Wonderful Wife. He felt he was returning to a second home for there were many people in the big city who had emigrated from Galicia, Andalucia and Europe generally in the previous decade. He would be among friends and, as he was to learn, his journey was worth every mile.

From letters he wrote to the family, to Professor Aragon and to others a remarkable picture emerged. Dona Vicenta told me "I think there were many who opened their arms to him. He was met by journalists when the ship called at Montivideo, and it was the same in Buenos Aires where many admirers greeted him, some of whom he already knew. He is staying in the Hotel Castelar on the Avenida de Mayo and says it is the best hotel in the city. Many were waiting for him there including journalists seeking interviews, photographers and friends. He is to give some lectures, and arrangements are being made for his plays to be performed."

Over the next weeks, as the news came through, it became clear that Federico was being treated like a true celebrity and was loving every moment of the adulation showered upon him. Blood Wedding, staged at the Avenida Theatre, received a standing ovation, but that was just the beginning. He directed 'The Shoemaker's wonderful Wife,' which also received rave reviews, and both dramas were played many times. Mariana Pineda, however, was not so popular, probably because of its political content. This did not seem to worry the poet. He basked in his success. His fame spread throughout the great city from Palermo to Caballito and San Telmo, and he was feted in the social salons and cafes in the Avenida de Mayo.

Among his many admirers were writers and artists including Girondo, Pablo Neruda, Ricardo Molinari and the actress Lola Membrives who presented two of his plays.

There was a second actress who was both his favourite and a good friend. This was Margarita Xirgo whom, although she had been born in Mexico he called 'the angel from Catalunia', and who had honed her theatrical experience in a theatre she founded in Barcelona. She was popular both in Spain and Latin America and counted Federica as her 'best friend.'

Sanchez told me later that he was astonished by the Press coverage of Federico's visit to South America. "It was not a question of column inches," he explained. "It was full page spreads plus photographs in the nationals and the Arts magazines. And it was not just about his plays. He is giving lectures, interviews, talks on the radio, attending receptions and parties where he plays the piano and sings his songs. He is becoming a national hero!"

According to Dona Vicenta he was also becoming rich beyond his fondest dreams. She said he was being so handsomely paid that he was able to send very considerable sums of money, and presents, home to the family. "He does not hide his pride. Now he is showing his father how a poet can earn a living! He does not need us to support him!"

It also became clear that despite the demands being made on him he was also finding time to continue his writing and was hoping to complete a new play called Yerma. He had written the first two acts, but not the third, and was being bullied by Lola Membrives to complete it. She wanted the new play for herself, for she had realised that when staged it could produce a small fortune for her. Federico, however, refused to be bullied, and did not complete the play until he was safely aboard his ship for the voyage home. He had intended to spend no more than four or five weeks in Argentina, but he also went to Uruguay. In Montevideo he directed his version of Lope de Vega's 'La dama boba' and gave lectures and readings which earned him even more money.

News of his success reached Mexico and impresarios there offered large sums if he would agree to bring his plays and himself to their theatres, a move supported no doubt by the actress Xirgu. He was busy and declined the invitations.. He returned to Buenos Aires with his version of 'La dama boba,' which the actress Eva Franco directed, and where Lola Membrives opened a celebratory offering at the Avenida with extracts from 'Blood Wedding', The Shoemaker's Wonderful Wife,' 'Mariana Pineda and two scenes from 'Yerma.' Then it was time to say farewell. He had been away for nearly six months and the family was urging him to return. It was March 1934 when finally he said a tearful goodbye to what he called his "Second Spain."

The family and some players from the Barraca welcomed him home when his ship berthed in Valencia. The actors had just returned from a successful tour in North Africa where 'Blood Wedding' was accounted a great success.

※※※

It was several weeks after Federico's triumphal return that Sophia started saying how much she wanted to see Federico's play. I assumed that she meant 'Blood Wedding' but she said "No, it is not that. It is a new play. The Rosales family told me. They have been to the opening in Madrid. I think it is another story about farmers and the peasants. It has a strange title called Yerma, and they say it is attracting much attention. I would like to see it."

There was again that look in her eyes which was becoming more and more familiar. Yes, her beautiful eyes that I had loved from the start. Green eyes. Wide eyes, often bright and sometimes dark, eyes that smiled and reflected every changing mood. And at this moment I realised they were communicating a very firm request.

"I really do want to see the play, Luis. The Rosales took the train. After all, Madrid is not the end of the Earth, it is not too far."

The eyes unmistakenly were saying please, and I was puzzled. In the end it was clear she felt so strongly that I had no choice. I said I would make enquiries

"Tomorrow?" she said. "Will you do it tomorrow. Promise. Just for me."

I promised, but it took a little time. First, the railway to Madrid. I heard that the line was being renewed. It would involve many hours travelling. And then the Teatro Espanol. I would have to make reservations. I mentioned this to my boss, and his office kindly discovered timings and costs for me. It would be an expense that I could not really afford but if I wished to retain the love of my 'green eyes' I would have to do it. And after all, I too wished to see Federico's new play. We would have to stay for the night in Madrid after the play, and that would mean more expense. Well, I just decided to stop worrying about the money. We would do it.

When I told Sophia I had made the arrangements she gave me a big, solemn hug. She said "If Federico is directing the play we can also see him! I would like that. After all, it is clear that he is now becoming a famous person!"

I replied that when the play ended we could try to see him and perhaps go to the Stage Door, no doubt with others who were friends and supporters. But I reminded her that Federico was now so well known that there was no guarantee. When people acquire fame they usually had their advisors, and also their protectors from the public. I conceded that we might be lucky compared with others, for after all, our visiting card was the simple fact that we knew him well, and he knew us.

Looking back, I realise there were very good reasons why we should not have made the journey to Madrid, but it is easy to be wise after the event. I had laid my plans carefully. When we reached Madrid we would first visit Professor Jorge Aragon for he had kindly said if I ever required accommodation I could stay with him. I had explained that with Sophia we were coming to see Federico's play at the Teatro Espanol and he had replied that he only possessed a small flat near the University but could find a bed for us. That was good and I accepted. What was not good was the journey. Sophia packed some bread, cheese and a bottle of wine because there would be no food on the train. The rail system was being improved. Well, I have to say improvement was needed. It was to do with moving from a wide gauge system to a narrower line, and we would have to change trains near the north border of Andalusia.

We were positive and hopeful, and we made good time. After two hours we were somewhere south of Linares. We had crossed the Quadalquivir near Vados and were approaching Estacion de Madrigueras when the train came to a sudden halt. Somewhere to our left towards the lower slopes of the Sierra Morena there were gun shots, not one but a distinct fusilade. They came louder and very near. Then there was shouting and the sound of rapid shooting, not a rifle but I think a machine gun. I was alarmed. Travellers in our coach leapt out of their seats and were peering from the windows. Sophia came beside me, seized my arm and was very frightened. The conductor from the back coach stamped his way past and called that we should keep from the windows and lie flat by the seats. We did not need telling twice. We remained there. And waited. Then the shooting stopped. Silence. No one spoke.

I held Sophia close and felt my heart jumping in my breast. We were terrified. Still we waited. No more shooting. Then the conductor came again and said we should take our bags and prepare to leave the train. It started to move very slowly until we reached Madrigueras and there, with the other travellers, we got out and crossed the line to another train.

We moved on from Madrigueras, still fearful because the train kept stopping. But we heard no more shooting. Eventually we continued on our journey, drank some wine and ate the cheese Sophia had brought.

We were never informed who or what caused the gunfire, nor whether anyone was killed, but it was later suggested that it was a Falangist gang hunting down a group of Republican politicians who were thought to be on the train, and were returning to the Cortes.

Such lawlessness was enough to scare anyone. We kept our heads down. And our fingers crossed.

The hold-up made us late and when, greatly relieved, we reached Madrid we had to go directly to the Teatro. There was a full House. A sense of anticipation and excitement. We recovered our good spirits. The play was styled as a tragedy with the action revolving round Yerma, her husband Juan who is a farmer, and Victor, a neighbour who also farms and is a shepherd. A bare stage and wonderful acting symbolised Yerma's moods of hope, of longing and despair. Her predicament was brilliantly interpreted by Federico's favourite actress Margarita Xirgu.

In the first Act it was made clear that Yerma and Juan had been married for two years, and it had been a happy wedding. As time passed Yerma longed for a child, but clearly Juan did not. He was unable or unwilling to give her one. He is seen as a good farmer and he is always busy with his olive trees and vines. Yerma complains that he is away in the fields too much. She wants him at home. She longs for a child. a son. She is torn because at the same time she feels she could be made pregnant by the virile Victor to whom she is strongly drawn. Her own conscience will not allow it and fear of such infidelity prevents her.

In the second Act there were songs and poetry, but also deep suspicion. Yerma goes out and about and her husband begins to believe that she is seeing another man, or even men. Meantime the village women continue to tell her that she should get pregnant, one way or another. There are plenty of men who could have her if she would allow herself to agree. But she cannot betray her marriage vows and live with the guilt that would haunt her.

In the third Act she allows herself to be taken to a mountain shrine by a peasant women, to work a spell which the other women vow will bring her a child. In the distance there is a fiesta. There is much music and dancing which serves only to heighten Yerma's terrible predicament. In the end her husband does come to her and holds her, wanting her. But by now it is too late. Hate is in her heart and as they struggle she attacks him. Agony consumes her. She seizes him by the throat and strangles him to death. Her misery contrasts strongly with the fecund village women, young and old alike who have advised her to get pregnant come what may.

The drama is powerful beyond belief and I could only marvel at the poet's skill and his uncanny insight into the heart and desires of women. I confess I was deeply moved, even hurt, despite the poetry and song, the colour and contrast, the music and dramatic lighting effects. The hand of a poet and dramatist of genius was everywhere.

At the final curtain, as Xirgu took bow after bow, I rose with the audience. Thunderous applause. Then, at first I did not believe it. I hardly noticed, but Sophia remained sitting until I pulled her to her feet. She showed no enthusiasm. She shielded her eyes and rocked to and fro until I thought she might fall. So I held her and saw she was weeping. Tears streamed down her cheeks. I did not know if Federico would be back stage, but even if he was Sophia was in no condition to meet him.

❋❋❋

Professor Aragon was as good as his word. He greeted us in his flat and showed us to our room.

"I regret it is so small and the bed is not big. But, if you open, yes, that door there it is not a cupboard. Presto! You see? It is a shower. I have all modern facilities! Now, when you are comfortable you may come through to me. I have jamon and a good bottle of Rioja, it is a Reserva. I think you may like it, and we drink to the great success of Federico Lorca. I have seen this play and would be interested to hear your opinion. I find it very advanced, and in dramatic terms little short of a revolution!"

His study was also his bedroom, but we sat comfortably as I told him first about the shooting on our journey in the train. He nodded.

"I can believe it. I fear there will be more disturbance. Even here in the city under the noses of the Army the International is being sung, yes, communists make parades with the clenched fist!"

I began to tell the professor about the performance of the play and how brilliant and agonising I had found it. But then I paused. Sophia made no comment. She looked pale and was obviously struggling, I thought, to stay awake. She would not accept a glass of wine and presently excused herself to go to the bedroom. Professor Aragon was as courteous as ever. "She is upset. I understand. It must have been very frightening on your journey. She will sleep and feel better tomorrow."

I realised that she was tired, and I too was weary and thinking of bed. The hour was late and I felt drained of emotion. A little later I excused myself and hoped Sophia might come back to the study briefly if only to thank the professor and say her goodnight. In our room I found she had not unpacked her case and was simply sitting on the bed, silent and still as if there was a weight on her shoulders. I was concerned and went to her.

"Sophia my love, are you alright?" I said, feeling stupid, for clearly she was not. "Come back, just for a little time. I am sure the professor will let me make you a hot drink if you would like it."

She shook her head. "I will be alright." But her eyes were red from weeping.

"It is the play that has upset you my love, and I understand. It is a tragedy. A drama. It was very moving, and very, very sad. It was wonderfully presented, but it is not real life."

"But it IS, and you know that!" She sounded angry rather than sad, and added "If you cannot understand you have lost your heart!"

I was shocked. Then, of course, how could I be so stupid? I saw clearly what had happened. She had slipped out of her skin into another. She had become Yerma whose agony we had just witnessed. The young wife who could not bear a child of her own, who could not cherish the one thing she, like every woman, craved above all else. Of course! And Yerma was not a real woman's name. I remembered now. It was a word meaning barren. Empty. And that was our own situation, not in a play, not a drama, but in reality.

"Sophia! Hush my love. No tears. I understand. We are unlucky, but we agreed. We had to. We accepted, and that was some time ago."

"No!" She dabbed at her eyes and sniffed. "It was yesterday."

"Listen, you know how we took all possibilities. The hospital. We checked and double checked. We did everything, and we managed. You, my love, have managed so well."

I realised now why she had been so keen to see the play. She must have heard its story from the Rosales. But it was the one thing we should not have done. It was not our journey to Madrid, it was the play that had been a mistake for us. Fate had played a malevolent trick. Sophia's sense of loss, of frustration and longing, had resurrected itself and most unjustly it was punishing her. We had no children but the fault was not hers, nor was it mine. Federico with his insight knew too much. And, for us, unhappily, in a matter of two hours he had shown us the bitter side of life and had presented it so forcefully.

I could have cursed the poet, but of course I did not. Genius will have its way. We should applaud inspiration, and we should try to accept what was inevitable, not condemn it. I was angry now. And so sad for Sophia, my very brave wife. Who, I thought, with the strongest of hands, could hold back the tide, even the smallest wave on the shore.

❆❆❆

The following morning the good professor asked kindly after Sophia and trusted that she felt better. She replied that she did, and I was greatly relieved. We had spoken much of the night and she, knowing there was no way of putting a patch on the past, accepted that to grieve was senseless. She apologised but I told her there was no place for the word 'sorry'. She again accepted her loss and for that I simply loved her the more. Our host, with some understanding, did not ask questions. Instead he offered his own reaction to the play.

"I found it remarkable, troubling, very moving, and the performances were of the very best. But that I expected. As a playwright Lorca strikes a chord in the drama unlike any other before him. As a poet the songs, also the music and even dancing are natural but also in a strange way they are both new and old.

"I would have to see the play again fully to understand what he is trying to tell us. He appears to be able to get inside a woman's mind and read her desires even though he may not understand them. There is a powerful display of anxiety, frustration and guilt. Is he displaying his own femininity and an obsession with infertility? He has always said that the theatre should be the place where poetry comes alive, but in this play there is much more than poetry. We see the many sides of woman-ness. He has much to thank his mother for. It was she, after all, who first taught him classical piano and encouraged his love of music and drama. In this play he had a very fine actress in the title role. Margarita Xirgu as Yerma enhanced her formidable reputation. I have to say the play was received with acclaim and pronounced a success by the serious critics and public alike. At the same time you know, not everyone was pleased."

He paused and was shaking his head "You will not have seen the newspapers after the first night. They reported that when the curtain rose there were boos and cat calls from the gallery, and insults hurled at Xirgu and at Lorca himself who had spoken briefly before the play began. There were shouts of 'Queer! Queer!' until those responsible were removed from the theatre.

"Several of the newspapers condemned the production out of hand. One in particular deplored the crude language and said the play was obscene. Unhappily, I suspect that the Church, with supporters from the conservative Right had orchestrated this simulated show of disgust. They were not going to applaud a playwright with known Republican sympathies, or a story that featured peasants and that pagan woman."

The professor's comments were worrying. Federico had never attempted to disguise his sympathy for the Republican cause, nor his gratitude to the government for supporting the Barraca's tours of the provinces. He always wanted his plays to be seen and appreciated by working people but denied that they were 'political.' For myself I realised there was indeed an inevitability about what he felt compelled to show us. As someone remarked, his plays, and particularly his poetry, were fired with an energy which stemmed from nature, from all that he had absorbed when very young.

He called himself a dreamer and a romantic, and although wellborn and from a comfortable home he was still a son of the soil of Andalusia, a child of Granada.

Many of his songs and ballads reflected what his countrymen experienced, not simply loss, frustration or privation but also the beauty of the *Vega*. He sang of the sunrise and sunset, roses, fountains, orchards, rivers, olive groves and the whisper of rain on small, hidden gardens. And, because he knew the lives of the *campasinos* so well he absorbed their passion and their struggle with adversity.

Part Six

Blood, Grief And Tears

He was an honourable man. A big man, and not simply in his girth. He was our new Mayor of Granada and to me he seemed fair-minded. He was a Republican, a loyal servant of the community. I salute Jose Ferdinandez-Montesinos. And I record this not because he was Federico's brother-in-law. I record this because that is the impression I receive of him from everyone who knows him and works with him. He is also a touch more cheerful and optimistic than Don Rodriguez with whom he has one thing in common. They both smoke the very best Havana cigars and, in my view, the Mayor makes sense whenever political affairs are discussed.

On occasions, at the day's end, we found time to exchange a few words. He spoke openly of Federico and, in his gruff, warm accent, freely offered me his opinion.

"Federico," he affirmed, "agrees with me. I would call him a Republican, but he seldom allows politics to hurt the imagination that is so *unico* in his plays and poetry. Maybe he is a bit of a fancy fellow? I admit it. I have advised him to take care. There are those here in Granada who openly dislike his ways and the manner of those who follow him. You understand what I mean?"

I nodded. I had heard Federico called *el maricon de la pajanta* (the Queer with a bow tie).

"Yes," the Mayor continued, "he must be careful. But, the family is very pleased and proud of his success. He celebrates the good name of Andalusia, of Granada, even of all our entire country before the rest of Europe. America as well." He grunted and added "Better than a politician!"

His face darkened. "But, we will not speak politics. It is now becoming impossible."

It was also becoming dangerous. There were those, including Azana, who said Spain was no longer Catholic, but they were wrong. There were still Monks and probably thousands of nuns and many religious communities still active. In fact, the Catholic Party, CEDA, was increasing its strength and influence just as an element of Fascism was also gaining supporters. The number of followers of the Monarchists also appears to be growing. And there are unusual happenings. Several who support the political Right in the Cortes have planned an Italian adventure and visited Mussolini who has encouraged them to strengthen their Party. He made alarming promises. It became known that for the Monarchists he would make available at least one million pesetas, thousands of rifles, 200 machine guns and 20,000 grenades.

When Sophia asked me which Party in the Cortes would succeed in winning and taking the reins of power I had no answer. We were no longer simply in a state of unrest, it looked as if we were to be confronted by yet more violence. The struggle for power lay in many hands, as the radio and newspapers reported in their attempts to cover the Government, the opposition's tactics and competing factions. It was not easy. There were mass meetings, and bloody encounters. Even murders.

My friend Sanchez said he feared the worst. He was no prophet, but he had access to news of events as they unfolded before we were aware of them. He spoke of reports coming through to his newspaper from many areas. I recalled that his people had successfully covered the on-going attempts at self-government by power-brokers in Catalunia, and also in Valencia. Several provincial councils in Catalunia had come together to form a government in opposition to Madrid. It sought to control communications, Law, public works and education. The attempt failed but it may have been one of the factors to influence a growing mood for change in the north.

It was feared that the entire country could become a State divided against itself. Reports showed that wealthy landowners did not like Azana and his Republicans. Nor did the Church. The Army, too, was becoming increasingly hostile, and political, and was fractured by conflicting ambitions. Despite its internal quarrels it was moving closer to the Monarchy. There were plots and counter plots.

"And now it is the miners in Asturias," said Sanchez. "They have always had permanent jobs, and a fair measure of power through their union. But now they have gone too far. They have come out on strike. It is said they number many thousands, and they are recruiting other groups, socialists, communists, anarchists and the *campesinos* who will gladly grab any opportunity which, they hope, will help them out of poverty and into a better life. Altogether the rebels, who probably number a formidable 30,000, are very well organised from their headquarters in Oviedo. They declare that 'those Fascists in Madrid' must be prevented from advancing their cause any further, and vow to create a new society for the whole of the country. They are preparing to take up arms."

In the Cortes Manuel Azana had been the War Minister. He made no secret of his dislike and distrust of the Church, and now it seemed he was not entirely enchanted by the Army. As a die hard Republican he was hell-bent on stemming the waning support for his Party. But he was being thwarted. In Asturias the rebels were reported to be organising committees and active groups with uncanny speed. Each township, from Gijon in the north to Mieres in the south had its own well established revolutionary cabal. Fighting broke out. Within several days of the uprising Oviedo had fallen to the Miners. "Long live the Revolution!" was the cry as violence overtook the entire province. The Monarchists, Fascists and the Church were declared targets. Convents, churches, Holy places, and the Bishop's Palace in Oviedo were burned down and priests as well as Civil Guards were shot. Fear, like an unchained brutal animal stalked the land, and even in Granada, as far away as any place could be from Asturia, we felt the tremors like an earthquake. The under-privileged, the hungry and the downtrodden combined with the miners and declared that they would prevent the nation from becoming a Fascist state. One earlier item of disastrous news, late but inflammatory, had spread like a fire: King Alonso had visited Rome to direct and to further what his followers advised against the Government.

With the violence escalating it was obvious that the government, now under siege, had to make up its mind. And quickly. It took a fatal step. At least that was what Sanchez called it.

"They are sending for the Army. In fact it looks as if they are relying on the Foreign Legion. Troops from Morocco, led by the former Brigadier General who commanded them, are being called in. I've heard of him before. General Franco. He is said to be a tough leader and very brave in the field, and there are those who also say he harbours political ambitions."

For us in Granada while it was becoming impossible to look ahead, I also had heard of the General Franco. He was one of the youngest among many Generals, and probably one of the most successful. He had been born in Galicia and knew Oviedo. He obviously had a lot of experience under his soldiering belt. Many considered him dangerous. Sophia and her friends were not uneasy, they were frightened, as were the men I met in the cafes who had not been called to arms. Dona Vicenta, thanks be to God, wished to reassure her friends and dispel their anxiety. Although she was a Catholic she was in favour of the Republican government and trusted it would survive the plotting and the threats.

In conversation I attempted to understand what was in her mind. What did she really believe? She said "There has often been trouble in the north. Some have too much money and too little religion. Others have religion but too little to eat. Here, we are fortunate, and must not worry. It is sad, yes, but we will say our prayers and we will have peace, because we look to our own families and care for our business. It is in our tradition. Revolution cannot come to Granada."

I felt less sure. I had spoken with her at some length and realised that privately she felt that if revolution did reach the streets of Granada all would be lost. The signs were not good. The leaders of the uprising in the north had plenty of arms and ammunition, they were well organised and profited from a wave of mass emotion. It was not long before the cry went up: "There will be blood, sweat and tears! Long live the revolution!" Every town in the province appeared to be ready to fight. And so they did. They had plenty of ammunition, but were no match for the legionnaires, the conscripts and the Guardia Civil combined. In the end it took three terrible months, but by October the General and his army proved too strong for the hot-headed, rebellious workers. Oviedo and Gigon fell and 'the Reds' were forced to surrender. The retribution was fearsome. Thousands were killed or injured and many of the leaders were imprisoned. In Madrid they were hailing the general from Morocco as the saviour of the nation.

✳✳✳

According to a letter from Professor Aragon in Madrid students, writers and artists had little time for Franco, they were much more interested in celebrating the success and praise that Federico was receiving. Now, back in his own country he was busier than ever. After the success of Yerma he was working on a new play and, at the same time was directing a longer version of 'The Shoemaker's Wonderful Wife' at the Teatro Coliseum. The Professor reminded me that it contained comedy, even farce, with a wife aged 18 cursing her marriage to a man of over 50. Federico was also staging his popular puppet plays which I had never seen. Don Cristobal had proved a great success earlier with its rough language, hilarity and the vulgarity of the puppets, all controlled by the puppet master himself. Maybe it was a style and form he had devised originally with Manuel de Falla. I said to Sophia it was remarkable that he possessed so much fun and such energy and commitment to an entirely new style of theatre.

"It is the praise and encouragement he receives," she replied. "I think he likes nothing better than to have his supporters around him, spoiling him and slapping him on the back. Such adulation must go to his head."

I was saddened by Sophia's tone of voice even though I realised what caused it. She would confess to admiring Federico's talents as a poet but found it difficult to accept his private life. I found it troubling as well, but I was not going to assume it would hurt his genius. I think it was now becoming more widely known that he had lovers, perhaps many lovers. He denied this, but without them his ability to create his ideas might not be so strong. One of his close friends was with him all the time. It was a student called Rafael Rapun who had joined La Barraca on its recent tour.

"Sophia *carino*, do not worry your head on this. Federico is someone who loves people. To love is natural, and it is quite clear that he loves women. In his plays there are always women and not so many men. He understands women and the problems they suffer. For him love is a constant theme."

"You are too soft Luis! In many of his poems, as you know perfectly well, his theme is more about death. I think that is not good. I would like it if he could be more cheerful."

"But he IS very funny at times. Are we going to have an argument?"

Yes, of course!" She came and put her arms around me and planted a kiss on my lips. "If we argue on something I know that you are there, you are alive and I also, but I do not like plays that talk of death. That is my last word!"

I held her close. Those green eyes! How I loved this woman. It was a miracle that we had met. It was chance. Or fate? I could not help this love, and I wondered again that she was so good to me, even in her sadness. How could an argumentative man like me be so lucky.

Part Seven

Like Dew To Our Souls

Federico was now spending more time in Madrid and his family are worried. They had been delighted with his great success in Buenos Aires, but the situation in Madrid was making us all uneasy to say the least. I am sure he was well aware of the political turbulence that was continuing to increase, and yet, according to Dona Vicenta, Federico was still hard at work.

"With his friend Rapun he is re-organising the plays for La Barraca, and the adaptation of 'La dama boba', and at the same time is writing a new play, giving readings and also directing the Shoemaker play at the Teatro Coliseum. It is always well received, but I think it is too much for him. He should come back to Granada and the family. We see so little of him now."

I said I thought perhaps he did not want to disappoint his admirers, indeed, his public. For he now had an international following. Quite apart from the Americas he was becoming well regarded by writers and poets and cultural groups in Italy, Portugal and England where, it is said H. G. Wells, among others, greatly admires his poetry. It was not long before his new play, which he had read to friends at the Residencia, was ready for rehearsal. It was to be premiered not in Madrid but at the Principal Palace in Barcelona. The radio and newspapers, so busy with reports and comments on the political situation, even found space to announce that Margarita Xirgu was likely to take a leading role in the new play.

I make no secret of the fact that I am constantly amazed by this former student of mine. I remember him saying "sometimes I find myself empty and can find nothing. But then there is a voice in me which sings and makes images I cannot forget." How could I have known he would develop such talent in drama and music, and acquire fame so early in his life. It made me feel proud to salute his genius, and now I dearly wanted to see his latest work. The problem was that Sophia probably did not, for she had been so unhappy with Yerma.

To mention my interest to Sophia would not be easy. I felt she would decline an invitation if I suggested we should see the play. Much as she admired his poetry and his songs she would not want to be upset again. My best course would be to devise a plan. I would take her for a special supper in town, and invite Sanchez and his attractive wife to join us. Then, over conversation I would find an opportunity to mention the play. I would say it casually and not be too insistent. If necessary I would tell a little white lie. I did not know what the subject of the play would be, but it would not prove too difficult to invent a story which might catch her interest.

※※※

The Carmello near the Cathedral was always said to be a good place for new ideas in food. I had never been there but decided that was where we should go and meet with Sanchez and his wife Rosa. Professor Aragon was in town for a brief stay and he said he would be pleased to join us. I thought the Carmello very smart. It was a *tapas*, a superior *taberna*. We found a table, and also a surprise, for there was Luis Rosales and his tall wife Carmen. I did not know her very well.

"*Mucho gusto !*" She had a Spanish nose and dark eyes but her hair strangely was silver with red streaks which I supposed came from a bottle!

"*Sorpresa! Sorpresa!*" she cried. "Why are you here?"

There was much delight, some kissing and hugging and then the Professor arrived. "*Hola!! Como esta usted?*" He hoped we were all well. I was pleased because we then put two tables together. We all chose, and I selected gambas with chilli and gengibre, chorizo e butiffara negra, and vieirus con serrano, also a plate of aceitunas and pan freco. Sophia chose a very decorative paella Valenciana and added a salada with asparrago e gengibre. The others seemed to be choosing atun or mejillones or salmon. We all agreed the food was experimental but very well prepared.

There was not too much talking at the beginning. We were hungry. Luis Rosales said "It is good that we meet, but we are not talking politics, it will spoil our food!"

"Good idea," answered Sanchez, "then we will not have a *pelea!*" (quarrel). He was aware that the Rosales had Falangist sympathies. We drank a few glasses of a new wine, Vilosell, which the Professor recommended. I think it came from Alicante, but I would have preferred a Rioja. I asked him not about the wine but whether the 'temperature' in Madrid had now settled down. He replied that he did not think we should talk of it.

I asked "You have news of Federico, or perhaps he is too busy with the plays he is producing? Is he not amazing? I understand not only does he write a play, he produces the play, directs the actors, designs the settings as well as the lighting and composes the music!"

"Well, he is busy with a performance of Don Cristobal, and also talking of a new play he has just completed. I do not know how he can do it!"

Then there was a stroke of luck Most unexpected. But now was my opportunity. I said that I would be very interested to see the new play, and added pointedly, but not looking at Sophia, that I did not think it would be like Yerma. "I have heard it is a comedy. Is that so?"

Professor Aragon shook his head. "Federico read some scenes to students at the Residencia, and they say it is entirely different, like a comedy of an early period. I think it is to be called The Language of Flowers and is set in nineteen hundred. That is all I know."

Rosa said "Then we must all go to see it when it is shown here in Granada!"

"Yes! Yes!" agreed Carmen . "What a fellow Lorca is, and now so famous! A star, I know he is admired everywhere. I do not like his politics, but I support him because after all I am married to a poet!" She pulled a face at her husband across the table.

"Of course!" replied Rosales. Then he took her hand. "But *paloma mia* his politics is not important, it is his music and his poems that are his wonderful gift. That is why we love him. You know this."

I was amused that Luis called her *paloma*, and felt with her long neck she was more like a *camello*! There was much laughter. I think she was becoming a little bit drunk. She was certainly enjoying her wine, and rebuked her husband.

"You poets are all the same, and I DO understand. But I like best Lorca's plays with puppets. I saw them when I was a kid, and even now I heard he has a new one called Don Cristobal which is very rude!"

"Well, it is different," commented the professor. "I have seen it. And yes, it is quite rude. He has called it a rural farce, but the puppets are not like his plays. There are bad words that the *campesinos* might use. It is down to earth, but not for polite society."

"You mean bums and breasts," laughed Carmen. "Well we all have them but, Holy Mother, we do not talk of them!"

Sanchez clearly felt it wise to stop the conversation, because he got to his feet and raising a glass said "We drink to Federico and success for his new play. Not the puppets, the one about flowers!"

We all rose and raised our glasses. There were four other tables across the room where several elderly people were seated. They had been eyeing us for some time and obviously overheard our conversation. Among them I noticed a young priest. He was about to get to his feet, but the man beside him pushed him back and himself rose. He pointed towards us and, more accurately, at the professor.

"You sir should be ashamed," he called. "We have heard enough of your poet and his vulgar friends. They offend the good name of Granada. We can do without such people!"

He sat down. The woman seated beside him turned in her chair and added in a harsh voice "He insults the Church. I do not forgive him, nor will the Holy Father! Your poet is notorious but he is wrong. He has a fine family but we do not want him here. He should go back to America and his fancy friends over there!"

Sanchez leaned across to me and whispered "I don't know her but I know the man. A lawyer." Jorge was shaking his head and said quietly "Take no notice, it is they who are vulgar, listening to our conversation." He was about to continue when Sanchez got to his feet again. He was swaying slightly and I suspected he had taken a little too much of the good wine.

Addressing us, he said in a voice that all could hear "The poet is no trouble-maker, he has genius. I do not forget I once met the head man on the Lorca farm, and his observation surprised me. I cannot remember his words exactly but the man said I sometimes think of young Lorca, the beloved child of our soil, as a bridge from old Espana to a new world. A bridge over the river of sorrow? No. He is the stream itself, the living water that has become like dew to our souls!" Sanchez paused, then added "Those were the words of a simple *campesino*, a good man speaking of a great man!"

There was silence. We were astonished. Not a word from the other tables. Then the Professor said "I can believe it! He reflects a truth of which I am sure. His songs and his plays are universal and can be understood by everyone, even by the *campesinos*. They have learned from La Barraca, the actors who open a wider world to them."

Our little party continued as more wine was poured and we disregarded the people in the corner. There was to be no confrontation. I silently thanked the Professor because Sophia took up Carmen's suggestion and whispered to me that she would like to see the comedy by Federico. It was a happy accident. Thanks be to Jorge Aragon, my little plan had turned out to be a success. The only problem was that Rosa was wrong. The play would not be performed here in Granada but in Barcelona. Later, when I spoke of this to Sanchez and told him I was tempted to go to Barcelona when the play was staged he advised caution. He said it was not a good idea to be travelling there. He was quite adamant.

"Barcelona? No. Not at the present time. The city is losing its balance. Those Catalans, as you must know, harbour much jealousy against big brother Madrid. There is not hatred, but equally no compromise. There is unrest. There have been uprisings throughout Catalunia and it is feared a grave situation could develop there."

I was disappointed, and Sophia even more so. But I respected Sanchez, He was not usually mistaken in these matters. I decided to take time to consider. There was no great hurry, and as it happened, in the following week reports came through that the new play would not be performed until Federico had the actresses he required, and several of them were performing in Madrid. Lola Membrives, never slow to miss a financial opportunity, was creating a remarkable record there by directing Blood Wedding, The Shoemaker's Wonderful Wife, and Yerma. Sometimes she staged two plays in one night. No wonder the actresses Federico required were not available! I could only imagine his delight at having three of his plays staged in the city at the same time! Fame indeed. And considerably yet more money to his name.

❋❋❋

Weeks later it was my turn to be surprised. On returning from the Council offices Sophia greeted me with a smile in her beautiful eyes and such a warm embrace that I wondered what I had done to deserve such affection.

"It is a secret. "She wrinkled her nose.

"I like a secret, "I replied. Especially if you tell it to me!"

"There is a price. I have started the soup for tonight. You must finish making it, then I tell you!"

Devil take it! What, I wondered, was the game she was playing. I was not enchanted. It had been so hot up in the office and I was getting bored. And tired. Paper work is not so interesting as teaching. I did not expect it but I was missing the classroom.

"I am not in the mood for making soup. I prefer secrets. So, tell me."

"No. First, the soup!"

I loved her dearly, but the one thing about Sophia I did not care for was that once she had made up her mind about something, in fact about anything, she was stubborn. Absolutely damned impossible. There was nothing for it. I washed, then started on the *zanahorias* and the *apio*. Then I sat down.

"There, now I am ready! What is this great secret?"

"Alright, I will tell you."

I don't know why she said it was a secret. She explained that she'd had a visit from Dona Vicenta. There was nothing very unusual about that. Dona Vicenta would sometimes visit when she came up from Huerta de San Vicente to buy flowers or call at the cathedral.

"Dona Vicenta told me good news. Federico is to come for a visit home and is bringing his new play!"

Her eyes sparkled and she jumped up from the table. "So you see, we do not have to travel all the way to Barcelona to see it, we can remain here in Granada!"

106

I was puzzled. I thought Federico was unable to stage his play because he lacked his usual team, his actresses, stage hands, carpenters, costumes, musicians and others who assisted him. They were all in Madrid. When I told Sophia there must be some mistake she denied it.

"If you don't believe me go and see Dona Vicenta. She was quite positive. He will come in ten days!"

I did not go to Don Vicenta. Federico came six days later. It was announced that the new play would not be performed. But, as he so often did, he would give a reading.

Part Eight

A Mutable Rose

The Teatro Isabel La Catolica in the high part of town is not as large as the splendid teatros in Madrid. Federico nevertheless had planned to take it for his reading. But he was thwarted for on the chosen day it was closed for renovations. The only other suitable place was the hall behind the theatre. It was hardly fitting for a celebrity performance. Federico was disappointed, but in the end he agreed it would serve his purpose. He was pleased to be on home ground, with time to share with those he knew and loved.

The hall had been equipped with a small stage. There was a proscenium arch painted gold and deep red curtains that do not rise and descend but draw to each side. It was a large hall, with a polished floor and separate rows of chairs. Here it was that Federico would give his reading After all, La Barraco had played in even more modest venues and he had raised no objection.

When the day came there was considerable excitement. Although not advertised in advance this was a very special event. The poet, always in great demand, was not now seen very often in the place he considered to be his true home.

With Luis Rosales and his wife, Sanchez and the Mayor and about a hundred others Sophia and I were in our seats in good time. The reading was to begin at seven. There were not many of the great and the good of Grenada present. Most of the seats were occupied by young people. I guessed that many were students from the university. Dona Vicenta arrived at the last minute. She had been driven up from the family home in an impressive Austin tourer and had a maidservant with her, and a driver who looked like the *granjero* (farm worker) who, I believe, was Don Rodriguez's usual driver.

Precisely at seven the lights in the auditorium dimmed and the curtains parted. There on the stage, brightly lit, was a row of chairs placed in a semi-circle in front of a black curtain. Immediately several figures entered and sat down. Each carried a folder. The two central chairs were unoccupied. Then Federico entered. Here was the man of the moment himself in casual dress, a loose tie at his throat. He too held a folder in his hands. We stood up, all of us rose, and we applauded. I thought he looked older than when I last saw him. He waved to silence us. We sat. With an exaggerated theatrical gesture he bowed then indicated the several others beside him.

"Good evening ladies and gentlemen!" he began, and I felt here again was the puppet master controlling the situation. "Should I say my lords, ladies and gentlemen? For here I see my honourable mama and the Mayor of our city! Now, before I begin I am pleased to introduce my little company for tonight. They are very fine actors from La Barraca and have agreed to help me. So here is Pilar, Miguel, Lola, Alejandro and Maria."

Each of them waved as he spoke their names. It was charming, but I was more struck by his presence. Something had changed. I thought he had donned a new cloak of maturity, but it was more than that. The moment he entered it was as if an extra glitter of light accompanied him, an almost uncanny glow, and it was not a theatrical follow spot. It was head-turning, commanding, compelling and brought a silence before he spoke again. His voice was deeper than before. It was an actor's voice, bold and colour-ful, versatile, and persuasive as if he spoke only to you individu-ally, telling you something important and in confidence.

"My main company that gives me such loyal support is in Madrid, as you may know." He paused. Then with a conspiratorial smile he added "Except for one. Tonight I have a surprise for you. Will you please welcome my dear friend and the first lady of the theatre of Spain, Argentina and Mexico, Margarita Xirgu!"

Another pause. Then on she ran from the wings to throw her arms around him, She waved a greeting and blew a kiss to us. Then the two of them stood side by side, hand in hand, as we thundered our applause. When we regained our seats they also sat, he in his casual suit, and she wearing a very smart black dress with a bright scarf at her neck and pretty red shoes. Sophia whispered to me "Look! She has such tiny feet!"

Federico began. "I have had this play in my mind and in my heart for perhaps 10 years, and now it is born. Can you imagine? I am pregnant for so long? I have to tell you that a poem is like a prayer. It arrives only when it wishes to arrive. And for me, a poem, a ballad, a song requires a theatre. That is what I have always believed ever since I was playing with puppets as a child. The place for poetry is the theatre. Only there can a dream, a vision, a poetic image become truly alive and speak to an audience, whether that audience consists of one or two people or many hundred."

He then explained that his new play was called 'Dona Rosita, the Spinster,' and that is was set in a villa in Granada. At that we immediately applauded and many stamped their feet welcoming the idea. When the thunder had died down the main characters, he said, were bourgeois "like many here in Granada," and they included the girl Rosita, an Aunt, an Uncle who loved flowers, a nephew, a housekeeper and a number of ladies who were visitors to the house.

"At the opening the period is the year nineteen hundred. At the end it is nineteen hundred and ten. In the play you can see this in the different dresses the women wear. There are three acts also showing the passage of time. Time passing is also seen in the flower most loved by the Uncle whose great interest is in flowers. It is the mutable rose which, each day, changes from bright red in the morning to pink in the afternoon and then to white as snow when the moon brings in the night. There are songs and dances and some comedy as you will hear. And now, we will read to you with the Barraca playing their parts. Please imagine a room with a conservatory where the Uncle is busy with his flowers."

Federico then turned to his little group. "You are ready? Then — curtain up!"

I found myself hoping that Federico would surprise us by sweeping aside the black curtain at the back of the stage like a magician to reveal, well, heaven knows what, but alas, no such treat. The reading began. I had never heard the several Barraca actors in action, and they were excellent, with Federico reading as the uncle and Xirgu reading the part of Rosita and also, very skilfully the amazingly vocal and outspoken Housekeeper.

After almost two hours, at the end I did not know whether to shout or laugh or weep. Sophia was silent and as white as the strange, mutable rose. There was prolonged applause. The curtains closed. A final surprise was to meet a man I had never seen before. Federico and the other players came among us as many wished to shake the great poet's hand. Federico stepped forward to embrace his mother and then turned to introduce Cipriano Rivas Cherif who, he explained, was Margarita Xirgu's Director. Then, without delay, the four of them left. The lights dimmed and the several Barraca performers drifted away.

We slept very little that night. Sophia kept waking. sitting up and asking questions to which I could not find an easy answer. "Why did you say it was a comedy when it becomes so sad at the end. It is tragic for Rosita."

"The Manolos and the Ayola girls are very funny."

"But Rosita is left alone, her lover never comes, only letters, and then her lost love marries someone else. After ten years she is a spinster, and the house is empty and left for sale."

"I think perhaps it is an allegory of life. The mutable rose is red for youth, pink for middle age and then changes to white for old age, loss, and death."

"I hate that! It is like Yerma, women who cannot have children. Why is Federico always making plays of loss, or loneliness or Death? It frightens me!"

"Come Sophia, we must get some sleep. Do not worry your head. The play was also great fun, wasn't it? There was comedy as well as sadness. We can discuss in the morning. I am sure the professor will have some answers."

I think she was emotionally exhausted, but eventually she slept. The problem was that I did not. In my own mind there were questions going round and round like a carousel. Why oh why Federico does your poetry so often speak a language of longing, of loss and death? I thought that perhaps only his violent muse spoke, and he himself could not give an answer. When next he came to visit the family in Granada it would not be easy but I would find an opportunity to explore this question with him.

Part Nine

Dona Vicenta Asks a Favour

The questioning did not resolve itself. The following morning at the Alcala Sanchez echoed my thoughts. "Remarkable play," he muttered, helping himself to an early brandy. "And an even more remarkable audience last night. Did you notice that many of our worthy citizens did not attend the reading?"

I understood his point. I said "The reading was not advertised, but even if it had been I think many would still have stayed away. They may appreciate that their son of Granada has become an international figure, but they are also aware that he no longer supports The Church, or the Monarchy. They know he is a Republican and some even think he is a communist! You see what happened at the Carmello. They were angry with him!"

"Yes, they are shocked. Federico no longer disguises his sympathy for the Left, but worse than that there is his noisy following, that crowd of homos. There are many good Church people here in Granada, especially the women, and they consider that crowd to be the children of Satan."

Immediately following the reading in the hall Federico had left for Cordoba with Margarita Xirgu and her director Cherif. Performances of his arrangements of two of Lope de Vega's plays were to be staged there. They then moved on to Barcelona where Yerma opened and received a tumultuous reception. Newspapers throughout the land were now generous with the space they accorded both Federico and the several companies that were performing his plays. Over a period of months he gave many talks and interviews and was lionised by cultural columnists, commentators, writers, and poets. When not giving a talk or a reading there was no respite as his supporters continued to organise celebration parties for him. More of his earlier poems and ballads were published, as well as his puppet plays. He also spoke publicly of his interest in Russia "that country of great artistic achievement, and the people's struggle for communism."

With Sophia and our friends I followed his movements from one city to another. It was, as one newspaper announced, like watching a meteor, a shooting star, travel across a cultural heaven. There was one fatality. The Barraca company, which had done so much to bring poetry and drama to the *campesinos*, was now disbanded. Federico had less and less time to spend with them, and their annual Government grant had dried up. As a consequence it left a number of talented actors out of work. Rodriguez Rapun who, when free from exams, had joined them was now able to stay with Federico in Barcelona for performances of Blood Wedding featuring Xirgu as the Mother, again directed by Cherif who also directed the premiere of Dona Rosita the Spinster. It was staged at the Principal Palace, and was an immediate, resounding success, lauded by the country's leading journals and newspapers.

※※※

Sophia was excited. "You will never guess. Today we have an invitation from Dona Vicenta. She asks that we go to her house, she says, for wine and conversation! Can you imagine why?"

I replied that I could not, but we should go. I had always liked Federico's Mama. She was a hopeful person, also kind and attentive to her church. And I liked her home. Huerta de San Vicente was white and clean, quite large and with a pleasant garden. Both she and her husband greeted us warmly. In the purple evening when it was cooler we sat to a table in the garden where a serving girl brought wine, olives, chorizo, *esparragos*, and *camarones* which were my favourite. How could she know! Don Rodriguez said "Well, Mister schoolmaster much has changed over the years since you came to see me about Federico's lessons on the guitarra. And now you work in the office of the Mayor?"

I said I respected my boss, but to be truthful I had enjoyed my teaching more.

Dona Vicenta nodded. "You gave my son a good start, and now he is famous! We thank you for being his good friend!" And she raised her glass. "We wish also to celebrate you! I think you said you are writing of his success in your journal?"

I replied that I felt it was important that a record should be kept of Federico's progress, and especially of his undoubted popularity overseas. "They worship him in Argentina, and even in England and in France academics are paying serious attention to his poems. They salute his genius. This can only help us. He is becoming our unexpected ambassador!"

Don Rodriguez nodded. "I agree. It is very good news. And now we have a favour to ask. You are aware of the situation I think?"

I said I assumed he was referring to the dangerous political malaise that was infecting the entire country. He replied that any hope of sanity or intelligent compromise was fast disappearing. It was very worrying. He said again "Governments no longer can govern!"

"No more of politics," interrupted Dona Vicenta. "I am thinking of my famous son. There is no secret of his friendship with the actress Xirgu. Well, you may know it has now been announced that she is to go to Mexico where her company will produce Federico's plays. She has asked that he should now go with her, or later if it is not convenient for him. Now, the favour we ask is that you can prevail upon him to go. We do not deny his intelligence when he speaks of his interest, and support, for the socialists. It is in his nature, ever since he was a boy. He wanted a better life for the poor in our land. He still speaks of it and says he wishes his plays to continue here for them."

"But the point is this," said her husband. "We have tried to persuade him to go, but have no answer. We believe he might listen to you.

We would like you to help him to make a sensible decision. Federico is not a politician, but he is making speeches and signing letters in favour of the Left. I would rather he concentrated on his plays. If, as I suspect, the present Government fails, more violence may follow, and those who support the Left, as he does, could be in danger."

Don Rodriguez's words came as no surprise to me. According to news reports Azana had just appointed Casares Quiroga from his Party to take the post of Prime Minister. Commentators were writing that he is not strong enough to stitch together the unhappy divisions among the Republicans.

It was a strange favour they asked of me, but I could not refuse. I replied to Don Rodriguez that I would try my best with Federico. "But, no guarantee," I said. "He is very confident of his position. He is his own master, and servant to no one."

"That is true," smiled Don Vicenta. "But I am sure he will listen. And you Sophia can make sure Luis will help. Now, we can finish the *camarones* and we will have more wine! We will drink to your success and to my famous son!"

We returned home in the darkness, as the cicadas became busy, and Sophia was in a dark mood. "You should not have been so soft, Luis. You know you cannot persuade Federico, he will do exactly as he pleases. He is now a very busy man. All the world wants him. You cannot blame him if his ear is to the world. It is only natural."

I could not deny it. He would not leave the country at this time, and I realised that there were different reasons, and one was that he would stay with his lover. Rapun was not leaving Espana. He was in Madrid. My problem now was that unless Federico came to Granada again, and soon, I could not speak with him. I decided I would write a letter, and give it careful thought. Two days later I did write and said the family were recommending that he should go with Xirgu to Mexico for a season of his plays. And I added that

I was sympathetic, as many were, to his support for the Left. But equally, I suggested that perhaps it was not the best thing to be declaring his interest in politics at this time, especially his support for the communist State in Russia.

❋❋❋

It was a week later when I received a reply to my letter. Federico wrote *'Luis you amaze me, but a little canary tells me that my Mama is on your tail. Is it not so? I have to be open to you. Madrid, j'adore! All my good friends are here and Pablo (Neruda) has appeared. I am also now completing a new drama of the very soil of Andalusia as I remember many situations on the Vega and the farm at Asquerosa. I am proud of my new play and will call it The House of Bernarda Alba. I will give a reading and I have an important role for Margarita. She is making plans for Mexico, that is true, but no, I cannot accompany her. For sure, I would like to go there later. When I was in Montevideo even then Mexico was asking for me. Now there is a dinner being given for me at the Hotel Magestic with many important people. I have to attend. Then Barcelona is asking for me to produce Dona Rosita at the Principal Palace, and I have given my word. Please kindly assure Mama and Papa that Mexico is my next excitement after Barcelona, and I will see them before I go.'*

The letter was simply signed (with a flourish) Federico. When I read it to Sophia she was not surprised. "He is right. You can see he is trying to keep hold of his life and with so many responsibilities it is very difficult for him. But I worry now he is famous, he does too much and cannot be everywhere."

He was always keen on celebrations with his friends. I realised that a genius lives in a different world to us and cannot be blamed. But I also feared that if he continued to make public utterances about his political preferences he could be running unnecessary risks. I was sad that I did not have good news to tell at Huerta de San Vicente.

Part Ten

Night Sleeper, First Class

Shortly after I received Federico's letter Xirgu left for Mexico while he continued in some state of excitement to read his new play to friends and newcomers in the Residencia. He declared that his play, a drama of a village family tyrannised by their dominating mother and denied personal and sexual freedom, was "pure realism." What was equally real at the time was that the Popular Front, a mixture of Socialists, Liberals, Communists, Trade Unions and Republicans and other supporters was divided against itself. There was animosity between the moderates and the more militant members. As a result it was losing ground rapidly against the Falangists, Monarchists and much of the Church.

All that Sanchez reported to me sounded grim. A state of emergency had been, or would be, declared. "It seems that Prime Minister Quiroga is of the opinion that, should there be an uprising anywhere it would pose no problem. He was confident that it would be quickly and easily repelled."

Unfortunately, the Prime Minister was wrong. Granada was now seething with trouble. Armed gangs stalked the streets. In Sevilla the Falangists took over the popular radio station and announced that a military coup was imminent. Even worse, Jose Castillo, a lieutenant in the Assault Guard which defended the Republicans, was shot. The following day, in retaliation, Calvo Sotelo, the Conservative leader in the Cortes was murdered. Violence, with senseless assassinations sent shock waves across the land. Federico was now well aware of the seriousness of the situation, and openly alarmed, he was driven to a state of indecision. On the one hand he felt he should stay in Madrid with his friends. On the other hand he thought it would be wise to seek safety with the family in Huerta de San Vicente. But would such a journey be safe?

His friends were in no doubt. "You must remain in Madrid," they said. "Or go anywhere, absolutely anywhere except Granada. There is serious trouble there."

The crisis changed from day to day. It was impossible to weigh up the uncertainties. He heard his friends repeated advice but they could not persuade him to calm down and stay in the Residencia with the students or with friends. He refused to even listen to that advice. Finally, on July 13th he made up his mind. He would return to the family. "I will go to Granada whatever you say. There I can be with the family!"

He packed a bag, said his farewells, and accompanied by Martinez Nadal who had attempted to hold him back, he went across the city to the station. There, fearful but determined, he bought a first class ticket and boarded the night sleeper to Granada. It was an uneventful journey and by daylight he was greeted by a delighted Dona Vicenta.

❋❋❋

Federico was no longer afraid. He was home, and back in town he had no hesitation in visiting friends and reading his new play to them. That is how it seemed. Sanchez told me "He actually called me to let me know he was back, and while he did not say it in so many words I suspect that he hoped my newspaper would report the glad tidings! I would have refused of course. He appears to have no under-standing of what is taking place almost literally on his doorstep."

"Are you serious? Surely he can see with his own eyes what is happening? The place is seething! I don't feel confidence myself crossing the street, and I am trying to persuade Sophia not to go out at present. You can trust no one."

Sanchez was deeply disturbed. "We're splitting down the middle. The garrison commander Suzman is a notorious Falangist, and the

Military Governor is General Aura, who as you probably know is a keen Republican. That spells big trouble."

"So you published not one word about Federico's return?"

"Not a whisper, Luis. You think I'm crazy?"

My good friend was far from crazy, but others were not. Somehow the word got out and the following morning the Catholic Herald put out the news that Federico was back in town. It was a front page story. Now everyone would know. And the news got worse. On July 18th in a broadcast General Franco declared that a National movement was being formed. He had thrown in his lot with the Falangists. Alarmed, Republican sources demanded that arms be distributed to the populace but Prime Minister Casares refused. Repeated requests were made. Exhausted, the PM resigned. Martinez Barrio attempted to form a coalition and failed. Two days later the town garrison here in Granada unexpectedly turned the tables with a terrifying result. They occupied most of our official buildings and arrested an astonished General Miguel Aura. To my dismay they also arrested my boss, Mayor Fernandez-Montesino. At the same time many more known Republicans were rounded up. Worst of all, there were assassinations below the walls of the Alhambra. The rule of Law, any kind of Law, had completely broken down.

Sophia was in a terrible state. She had heard from Alicia's family that the Albaicin was attacked. The gitane had done their best to protect their homes by digging trenches, but their labours were of no avail. The entire district was overrun. The defenders had few weapons and were no match for canon and grenades.

"I cannot believe it, Luis. It is terrible! There were aeroplanes shooting and bombing and many good people killed!"

We were terrified. I had narrowly escaped, and was fortunate in having left the council offices just before the Mayor was taken.

Now, we did not even consider venturing out. We were trapped. There was only one piece of good news. It seemed that Federico had at last got the message. He ceased giving readings of his play and wisely remained safe in Huerta de San Vicente.

Gangs of thugs walked the streets, but it was impossible to remain indoors indefinitely. If we were to eat I had to take a chance and get to the shops. Sophia said I should wait till all was calm again. I knew in my heart that calm was a long way away. I took my chance. If necessary the Alcala would be my refuge. Many shops were closed but the Alcala was open and so was the *tendero* two doors along. There, I met Sanchez.

"Good God man!" he cried. "Go home!" The Falangists will know that you worked for the mayor. They'll be out to get you!. They've already collared half your colleagues!"

He was right. I needed to be invisible. I made hurried purchases. as did Sanchez. Before I bolted back he said "Luis, you have to get away from here. Seriously, don't wait for trouble. Your best plan is to get down to the Genil, the Vega, get to the *campesinos*. There it is mostly Republican territory, and you would be safer."

I did not wait to argue. When I told Sophia she agreed with Sanchez. "Yes, he is right. And I have a thought. Maybe you could speak with Don Rodriguez. He will have many friends down there and they could hide us. Or there is Luis Rosales. He has Falagist friends. Perhaps he could get us there safely?"

I debated long and hard. I did not want to run, or be seen to be a coward. But to be invisible was clearly the best course. To disappear was only sensible. Two days later, an unexpected plan was offered to us. Don Rodriguez sent a message. He said he could not persuade Federico to leave Granada, he insisted in remaining in the house. But he recommended that it would be wise for us to leave without delay. Federico had the safety of his family, but we were too exposed. He wished to help us.

"They have taken the mayor. Next they will come for you. You still have a chance. Tell your good wife to meet with me at the house of the Rosales family, there she will be safe. The brothers are Falangists. I will instruct her. She must come alone. The street gangs will not harm her, she is Portuguese, not political."

It sounded like suicide to me, but Sophia said it was all that we could do.

"Sophia I cannot allow it! There is too much danger. Those villains will not respect anything or anyone, you know that."

"Luis, Don Rodriguez has influence, the Falangists cannot afford to harm him. It is more likely they would like to get their hands on Federico. But not the farmer. I will go and find out his plan."

I was defeated, I had no answer, and soon I believed I would have no wife. She insisted it was our only way. I had to let her take the chance, and prayed to God she would not be harmed.

We waited until it was dark. Fortunately there was no moon. It was not far to go. And with luck the streets would be quieter as most of the gangs were in such cafes as they could find still open and were busy eating and getting drunk.

It seemed an age, but thankfully Sophia did not take as long as I feared. She reappeared and I thought I must be dreaming. She was a heroine, I could not believe her courage. She was very pale, also breathless and now she was trying to comfort me. I found for her a glass of wine, and asked what Don Rodriguez had said.

"He was so kind. He said this is the plan. Tomorrow night, by midnight, we must leave the house and go to the cemetery, the one that is just below the Alhambra. There is some shelter there. There are trees. We must hide, stay very quiet and wait."

My mind was spinning. But NO! That is where there has been shooting. It would be better to go into the Alcazaba, yes and walk through to the Court of Myrtles, to the pool that reflected the stars, to the place where young women used to go in search of a lover, and there we could hide.

Sophia said that was no good. She was not going to listen to me. "Don Rodriguez says we must wait quietly by the wall in the trees. A car will come. It is the one belonging to Cisco, his driver."

"And he will take us to the Vega?"

"No, that is what I thought, but Don Rodriguez said he had instructed Cisco to take us away from the city. He would drive us to Malaga."

"Malaga? God in Heaven! How can that be safer than here in Granada?"

"Luis, you will be patient, please, I do not know if Malaga will be safer, and Don Rodriguez said he did not know, but it is the best way. He gave me the keys."

What could she be talking about. Keys? For what? I did not believe this.

She explained that Don Rodriguez said for the family, nephews and cousins and their children, there is this villa in Malaga where they stay for holidays. It belongs to all the family. "Usually they go there in August, but in this August no, of course they cannot. So Cisco will drive us there he said, and we could be invisible. I have the keys."

I had a vague memory of hearing years ago that the family possessed a villa that they used for holidays, but I thought it was in Madrid. I had no idea it was in Malaga. And even if there was such a place by now the gangs would probably have taken it, or even destroyed it.

"No, it is not destroyed! We have to obey what Don Rodriguez says, Luis. It is very kind of him to help us. I think we have to trust him. There is nothing else we can do."

"We have to go tomorrow night?"

She nodded. "Midnight. And we can take only one case each."

Part Eleven

La Paloma Blanca

No day had ever seemed so long, or the hours so slow. The hands of the clock in the hall seemed hardly to move. I had never waited for midnight before, and now I faced a midnight I dreaded. From dawn the sun had blazed. By mid-day the temperature must have been nearly 37o C. It was not until darkness fell and the air cooled a little that we found the energy to spread a few sheets over the furniture and put our best china and some silver in a drawer and lock it. We moved slowly, heavy-limbed as if trudging through a ditch of mud on the Vega below. It hurt to see my Sophie wipe the tears from her eyes. Were we in a dream? She tilted her chin, she was *valiente* and her love even then embraced me. I praised her. How I admired her courage. We tried to eat a meal, but I had no appetite. I was sick at heart. Upstairs we packed two bags and waited and my head was empty of words. We were leaving our home not knowing when we might return for it was clear we were now in a war and the future was a wall on which, if it bore a message, I could not read it.

It was the bells of St. Nicholas that I heard. I counted to twelve. Across my nightmare mind flew a black cloud of birds. I remembered Sanchez saying that when those bells rang it was a *Presentimiento*. A premonition.

A quick look from the window. The lamps showed an empty street. We lifted our bags, locked the front door and made a run for it keeping close to the walls of houses that I knew but which now seemed unfamiliar, like houses of another place. No-one was moving. A terrible silence. We saw no one. Then we heard singing and laughter some distance away. Those gangs. Assassins in a cafe somewhere, no doubt taking a brief holiday from killing. Before I died, if I had to die, that laughter would send me to my grave. We gained the walls of the Alhambra without incident. Luck was with us. Breathless, we crouched at the entrance to the cemetery and waited. It was Sophie who spotted it first.

"There, you see?" she breathed. "By the two poplars. I am sure. A car."

"Wait!" I took about ten paces. The darkness was like a blanket but between the leaves I could see better. I think she was right. If it was the wrong car we were dead. Then, I heard the voice of Cisco.

"Climb in. Immediante! We go now! We have ten minutes to be from the streets."

❊❊❊

I was not certain but I think it was a new road passing by the sierra, not the one we had once travelled on the way for our holiday by the coast. In the darkness we could see little and Cisco was not wasting time. The air cooled as we passed up a steep road, still climbing. I could see small points of light, pueblos. Zubia. Or Otura in the Reserve. We were in the land of the great Mulhacen where the lower slopes, as I knew, were the best garden in the world, so rich in flowers and fruits. Almonds, olives, grapes, apples and cherries. And the air made sweet with the scent of juniper, or thyme, or maple. I said, to comfort Sophia "We look forward, not back like the Moorish prince. Remember professor Aragon. He said the prince looked back to see the Alhambra he was leaving for ever. And he wept. This was his road of tears."

Beside me Sophia turned and replied "Even so, I am looking back."

We did, but in the blackness we could see nothing. Darkness. No lights The great Alhambra had disappeared as if it had never existed. But, we were not leaving for ever like those Arabs. We would return. I took Sophia's hand. "When this violence is ended," I said, "I promise we will come back to our home."

It was many kilometres. A long way to Malaga. Sophia slept a little. She was exhausted and worn with anxiety. The sky lightened as we approached the coast, and it was four a.m. when we reached Almunecar. Cisco said little. He was a man given to long silences. I dozed, but heard him say, "We go by Nerja and Torre. Very good fish."

The sun climbed at our backs and soon illuminated some white buildings that were quite tall. I think I saw the tower of a cathedral. At last, Malaga. I guessed Cisco had been here before. He knew his way, and when I asked him he nodded. "Yes. Many occasions."

We drove higher some way behind the streets and stopped at large wrought iron gates on which in stylish letters a sign read La Paloma Blanca. Cisco climbed stiffly from the car and producing a key he opened up the gates. He gestured towards an *avenida* and said "It is here. You have some keys I think?"

We lifted our bags from the car. I shook Cisco's hand warmly and thanked him. I said it was a good journey, a fine taxi and he was *experto*. Then I asked *quanto cuesta?* He answered. "250 pesetas". Astonished I said "Cisco, that cannot be enough!" He answered "For the gasolina. That is all." I paid him without delay, and as I did so he handed me a package. "From the family Lorca. It is for you." As he climbed back into the car he called "Suerte! Hasta luego!" (Good luck! See you later). Before he reversed and turned I asked him if he was going to drive back to Granada. He shook his head. "I go to Nerja now and then in the night I return, but to the Vega only." He explained that he had a son living in Fuente Vacueros by the Genil and he would stay with him until Don Rodriguez called him back up to the Huerta de San Vicente. We waved him goodbye, and I prayed that he would also have luck, and that we would meet again.

Humping our bags we closed and locked the gates behind us and set off along the *avenida* past palm trees towards a square, white villa. There were arches facing a lawn of parched grass.

I paused. And stared. "Sophia my love, here is our new home. Look! It is so large! What do you think?"

She also stared, wide-eyed. "It is a palace!" Perhaps not a palace, I said. But it looks very much bigger than I had thought. And so it was.

Finding the main door I turned the key in the lock and we entered a cool hall paved with blue and white tiles. My legs felt weak. My head was buzzing. We embraced. And we stood a long time holding each other, unsteady and nearly falling. Sophia, my lovely Sophia! Her cheeks were wet.

"If it is not a palace," she said dabbing her eyes. "It is a heaven, and the Lorca family I think, are angels."

Then, we explored. And we discovered that 'heaven' contained a spacious sitting room, a dining room and kitchen area, three bedrooms on the ground floor and two more upstairs. On the flat roof, a terrace looked out upon a woodland park. It was hard to believe, but we appeared to have a family mansion all to ourselves. A very beautiful new home! We unpacked our cases, and in a spacious bathroom we washed away the dust of the long road to the coast.

"La Paloma Blanca, it is a good name," said Sophia. "I think a white dove is a sign for peace."

"I would like to believe we will have peace," I replied. But I fear that is only a dream."

Her face clouded and I wished I had not spoken. "Come along," I said. "I'm hungry, we should go out and find some food. We will take care and I am sure we will find somewhere." Then I remembered the parcel Cisco had handed to me from Don Rodriguez. I would bring it with me.

Sophia was unsure and held back. "How do we know if it is safe to go down into the streets?"

I said we again had to take our chances. There were plates and cups in the cupboards, but I could find no food in the house. We should get to a shop or store and if nothing else we should buy bread and milk and some meat. I persuaded her that we would take every care.

By noon it was airless and the sun hurt our eyes. Thankfully we found the streets were quiet. The citizens of Malaga were hiding indoors. I could see why. In several streets it looked as if there had been an earthquake. A line of houses had been completely reduced to a pile of rubble. Not many motors were passing and few people walking. In the first Tapas we came to we ordered Aceitunas Alinadas, also *queso* with a bottle of wine. It was good, very good, and at last a smile from Sophia. The place was deserted, but I asked the girl at the Bar where we might buy some provisions and she said the best shops were in the area of the docks and we should go there. But, she added, it was not good to be walking the streets. We should be careful. There had been many deaths. Churches and houses had been burned. She crossed herself. "But now we are waiting. We are wounded but not destroyed. We are a sleeping tiger!" She clapped her hands. "Bang, bang! We will explode the enemy!"

In a market by the docks we made good purchases. Enough to eat for several days. We found fresh vegetables and fish. At an *arnicero* (Butcher) there was plentiful jamon. Sophia said "Now, we are more at home I will make sopa!" She was very pleased. I was also very relieved, but I was anxious. There was something sinister about a fine town being so silent as if unaware of what was happening in Granada and other towns in Andalusia. Or was it the reverse? Perhaps the people of Malaga were only too well aware of what was happening to their brothers and sisters in the north and feared it could be their fate too.

On returning to the villa, and after taking care to lock the gates behind us, Sophia said "Luis! What are we thinking? I have just remembered. You said you brought the parcel from Cisco to open, but you did not. Is it still in your bag?"

It was. We went through to the kitchen and I tore off the parcel's paper wrapping. Inside was a box of a dark sweet-smelling wood with small inlays of golden leaves. It looked like an expensive case for cigars. With it was a short note on headed paper bearing Don Rodriguez's signature.

Excited, Sophia snatched it from my hand and read "Take good care of my house. Here is a little something. My wife says may God be with you."

She stared at me. "What can it be? Shall I?"

I nodded and she carefully folded back the lid. Then reaching into the box she withdrew her hand and exclaimed "Mother of Mercy! Look!"

It was more than a little something. It was money. I counted out seven thousand and nine pesetas.

Part Twelve

A Bed of Olives

I gave the money to Sophia. "Housekeeping," I said. But I could barely believe it. Perhaps God was indeed with us. But if not, the amazing generosity of Don Rodriguez certainly was. I had brought my savings with us not knowing how long our money would last. It was pitifully small. Now, the gift from Don Rodriguez was manna from Heaven. Sophia simply stared. I could not read her face. "What can we do, we can never repay Don Rodriguez! He is so kind. How can we thank him?"

The answer was that we could not. Perhaps never. We were, for better or for worse, isolated, as if on a far island. But I was thinking constantly of the family. Of Dona Vicenta whom I admired so much. And of Federico. Was he safe, was he hiding? I saw him clearly in my mind as he was reading Dona Rosita, and how much affection he showed to his Mexican actress Margarita Xirgu. If you had to be part of someone's family I felt I would be proud to be a relation of Lorca.

The following morning I was sitting out on the terrace at the rear of the house preparing to make some notes for my diary when I heard Sophia call. "Luis, you had better come quickly! There is someone at the gate!"

I went down and saw there were two figures standing there. One carried a rifle. I did not like the look of either of them, and told Sophia to go back into the house. But she refused. "I stay with you."

One of the two was a rifleman and wore an Army uniform. His companion was clearly from the Guardia Civil. This could mean trouble. I asked them what they wanted.

"Open the gate !" demanded the rifleman. "It is official."

I took a deep breath. "This is a private house of the Lorca family." And I asked again what they wanted.

"The Colonel Luis Villalba demands that he should see you. We take you to him."

I shook my head. Sophia grasped my arm and whispered no. I answered to the rifleman "I do not know this Villalba."

The gun was pointed at me through the bars of the gate. "I say that soon you will, my friend. I think it better you come in one piece, eh?"

The civil guard growled. "You cannot refuse, it is an order from the commander."

"Open this gate!" demanded the rifleman. "Or I shoot."

I told Sophia to go and fetch the keys, and not delay. She ran, and when she returned I unlocked the gates. The rifleman shouldered his gun and took the keys. We were then seized and roughly bundled into an open car parked round the corner. We were driven swiftly, dangerously down into the centre of the town and came to a halt at what I imagined was the headquarters of the civil government.

"Don't worry," I whispered to Sophia. "This does not look like a prison." She was trembling and I was not much better. It was clear we were to face some sort of interrogation, and that was bad news. The car turned into a narrow archway and we were ordered to get out. With the rifleman's gun at our backs we were marched to a flight of stone steps and pushed ahead. We entered a square hall. I noted that there were no windows. To the left was a door bearing a decorative shield of what looked like polished bronze. The rifleman rapped on the door and a voice shouted "Entrar!"

This was certainly not a prison. We were in a richly-furnished room. On an ornate desk was a file of papers and two telephones, and behind the desk lolled the figure of a young man in an immaculate officer's uniform, with his booted legs on the desk top. Extracting himself he got to his feet and exclaimed "Ah! The Paloma! So we have TWO little doves! You have searched them?"

The rifleman who was standing behind us answered, "Not yet, sir."

"Idiota! Do it!"

We were both roughly frisked. The rifleman then saluted, turned and left the room. The young officer paced to a window and gazed out. Then he swung round and barked "Who are you, and what are you doing in that house?"

Brisk as it sounded it was the voice of a cultured person. As he spoke, poor Sophia who had been shaking uncontrollably slid to the floor. I stooped to help her. The officer shouted "Guard! Water!" It was a civil guard who entered. "Bring water for the little dove!"

The guard returned and handed a glass to the young officer. I was supporting Sophia in my arms and to my amazement he strode across and bending down pushed the glass to her and waited until she had taken a sip. Then he nodded to me. "Bring that chair. She may sit."

This was not the interrogation I had feared. "I have to trust," the officer began, "that you do not represent a danger to my town. Yes, my town. I am the Commander of Malaga Garrison. I have strong militia. All good men and faithful to the cause."

A theatrical pause. "But who, I ask myself, are you? Why are you in the Lorca house? Have you not one of your own?" He laughed. "I assure you I have a different house for you, but it is, should I say, not so fine as the Lorca and is already occupied. By a family of rats. Now, you will give me your name please!"

I replied that I was Luis Castejou and with my wife we had permission from the Lorca family to stay in La Paloma Blanca. We had come from Granada only a week ago. On hearing this he said "Why should I believe you? Maybe you are telling me lies? I must warn you this is not a time to be so foolish."

I thought that he seemed very young, but noted from his uniform that he had the rank of Colonel. Obviously he wished to display his superiority and intimidate me. But now it was my turn. I remembered I still possessed the note Don Rodriguez had sent with the pesetas. I took it from my pocket and handed it to him. He studied it in silence, then looked up. "This is a forgery?"

"Sir, with respect, even the best forger in the world would not stay in Granada." I explained that the garrison had turned and there were gangs of assassins seeking all Republicans and their supporters. The people of the town, civil servants, teachers, doctors, even women were being taken. " Many are murdered. It is no longer our Granada. Beneath our streets the Darrio runs with blood!"

He returned to his desk and sat drumming his fingers by the telephones. I thought he was going to lift a phone, but then he appeared to change his mind. "You are telling me that you know Rodriguez?"

"Yes. The family. They see us as friends. It was his driver who brought us to Malaga for safety."

He laughed. "Safety? He is joking!" Then his whole attitude abruptly changed. "You will know Federico?"

"Yes, I was his teacher."

To my great surprise he rose and came to me and held out his hand. "Please, my mistake. At this time we have to discover who is a friend and who is not. I also know Federico. Two years ago he was in my new car driving in Granada. I am a great admirer of the poet. And La Barraca. It is still performing?"

With great relief I shook his hand. "They were last in Santander but are now no longer performing. La Barraca is finished. The Government has no money for them, and sadly it is now too dangerous."

The young Colonel called for the rifleman and told him to hand the keys of the villa back to me. "Now mister schoolmaster I can allow you to return. I advise that you remain in the house. Have great care of your little dove. You are a lucky man, *e bonito*!"

As we were about to leave he said "You must understand the situation. You are fortunate not to be here some days ago. There has been destruction in my town. Perhaps you have seen this? It was from the sea. A gun boat. Many shells, but we could do nothing, I have no artillery. I must warn you, there may be more. We must hope for good luck."

❋❋❋

I reflected that, in a time like this luck was to be greatly prized. It was worth more than all the money in the world. Yes, I was lucky with my 'little dove', who would not be? And we were even more fortunate with the young commander of the garrison. He spoke with an accent that was upper class to my way of thinking, and he was clearly a Republican sympathiser. With great relief we hastened back to the house and made sure to lock the gates.

It was several days later that the rifleman appeared again with a message that I should accompany him to the garrison headquarters. This time, no gun was pointed. He said "It is not necessary for the lady. Only you."

I told Sophia not to worry. She was to remain, and I would soon return. Thus it was for the second time I found myself facing the Colonel. When we had left him he gave a smile. He appeared friendly and wished to assure us he was not our enemy. But today he was not smiling. His young face had a serious look. He pulled up a chair and bade me sit.

"You must know in politics much of my town is of the Left. The Partido Communista Espanol holds the most votes here. But not everyone is our friend. Already we have had houses burned. There is always some opposition. In the Cortes we have Bolivar. He was clearly elected and has strong support, but I fear it does not help us. Here I have ten thousand militia, but I am short of rifles, I have no canon and ammunition is low. Bolivar said he would arrange for me to have supplies. We have waited and had hope. But today I have received a message that it is not possible. The supplies have not come and I fear it is now too late."

"This is very serious?"

"No, it is disaster. Sevilla has fallen, and the nationalista is reported to be driving south to us here at the coast. They are supported by Italian bastards who care nothing for our country. They are Fascista, now paid by Franco. How am I to protect my town? I have militia, brave men, but with a shortage of ammunition it may be impossible!"

His next information was alarming. He said Malaga would fight, there would be much blood. He had little hope of success. There was danger and no time to lose. He said he wished to assist me and the little paloma to escape the fighting but there was little time.

"I have arrangements with the marine. I am the owner of two boats in a small company of coastal traders. Tomorrow you must get to the port and there enquire for the master, Humberto Leon. He is a good man. You can rely on him. He continues with his duties and tomorrow is leaving with a cargo for Morocco. He will take you and you will be safe."

Opening a drawer in his desk he took out some papers and handed them to me. "This bears my name, my shield of arms and my instruction. The captain will expect you and you will leave this shore. I do advise it. If you remain I cannot do anything for you."

I replied that we would rather remain and take our chance. After all, the villa was not in the streets of Malaga itself, we were on a hill. There was woodland there and much cover.

"That is foolish. You want to die? I cannot allow you to remain. You must go, even for the sake of your wife, it is madness for you to remain. You have no idea of those Italian bastards and what they do with women! I have reports as I have said. There are enemy brigades driving from Sevilla, also Ronda, and the numbers are great. Tanks, also artillery."

His instructions were brief. He had ordered two of his militia to call at the gates tomorrow before noon and escort us to the port. We must be ready. I wished to say more but he would not listen. We shook hands and I thanked him. Then with sadness, and fear, I left him. The commander was clearly a brave young man, no doubt a good man sensible of his duty. But from all he said I feared there would be little or no future before him.

Back at the house with my news Sophia, as I expected, became upset. We argued. "No Luis, we cannot go, we are better here, we lock the gates and shut ourselves in the house and can hide."

"Sophia, *carino mia*, churches and houses here have already been destroyed, blown to pieces! We will be dust and ashes. When the enemy attack comes nowhere will be safe. The Colonel says the town will fight to defend itself but it has not the armament to repel a big force. Colonel Villalba has made it quite clear. He wishes our safety. He does not want responsibility for our death, he already has too much for all of Malaga. We are to pack our cases and take some food with us."

"But how can we be safe on the ocean? And where will the boat take us?"

"I think he said Morocco, where we could try our luck. But we have to leave. We have little choice and even less time." I thought we should pray for the colonel. He wished to help us while he was still able to do so. Further delay could be a disaster. I went immediately to pack my case. Poor Sophia followed. She was very upset but did as I told her.

※※※

At noon the following day the two militia arrived as arranged. In a motor they drove us to the Port. Already there were boats of various sizes preparing to sail. At the customs we found Captain Humberto Leon. He had been informed of our coming and, accepting the papers I handed to him, he said the commander had given him instructions. He was large fellow, built like a barrel, with a weathered face, bearded and although not smiling he did not appear to resent our presence. He had a crew member with him called Telmo who looked little more than a boy, and it was he who, in due course, took us aboard the coastal trader. It was not large. Timber, also trees still in leaf, were being loaded on the deck. The vessel looked new, with a white bridge and cabin at the stern and a crane, or derrick towards the bow. The name of the boat was painted on the side. *Esperanza.* (Hope). I pointed it out to Sophia but it did little to cheer her.

I was not particularly cheerful myself. Telmo showed us to a dark cabin below the bridge with one porthole. It contained a narrow bunk bed. I asked if there was not a larger cabin. Humberto grunted. "You are fortunate to have this. There is no other for you. This is the cabin for my crew. Now Telmo will have no bed. My vessel is for merchandise, not persons."

When I asked if there was not another place I could sleep, he answered "The floor. We carry only olives and timber. I will arrange for some sacks of olives to make a bed. You can then get a good sleep. We sail at ten hundred hours."

He turned abruptly and left. Sophia was distressed. "It is madness! We should not be on this stupid boat! What are we to do?"

138

I replied that what she should do was to climb on to the bunk, say her prayers and try to get some rest. I would wait for my bed of olives on the floor.

❊❊❊

When the vessel cast off and we left the quayside and headed from the docks I had no idea how long we would be at sea. It was dark. No lights allowed. Several sacks of olives were brought with a rough blanket. I lay and listened to the beat of the engines and slept a little. I was heartened when, soon after dawn and a mainly sleepless night, we were shown below to a galley with a cooker, a small table and bench. There would be food, said Telmo. I doubted it but I was wrong. Breakfast consisted of sausages with bread, eggs and raisins. All this with a mug of hot coffee! Humberto came down as we were finishing, and I thanked him. We had not expected food.

It was a calm crossing until we were approaching Tangier. Humberto warned us that we might encounter rough weather. We did. Poor Sophia was suddenly quite sick. Humberto was unworried. He said "Here is always a bit difficult for all ships. It is the wind from the north west and Atlantic. Big waves!"

He was correct. We stayed below until Humberto had managed to guide us into quieter water and get alongside Quay Number Two for off-loading the cargo. It was now evening when we docked. The timber was to be un-loaded first. I said to Humberto that we would hardly be welcomed in Morocco, thinking of the recent history of violence there, but he said there would not be a problem because the freight we carried was much in demand.

"The timber we have is yew tree. The dried leaves are used to make a medicine that is much needed. It is a valuable crop. The hard wood is required for special construction. Then we take the olives to another place because I have to return with salt." He added that we could gather our cases and get ashore as soon as we wished. I said a silent goodbye to the olives. They did not make a very comfortable bed. Then I thanked Humberto for a safe passage, and out of interest I enquired where he would go for the salt. To my surprise he answered "Olhao, of course." With a shock I realised he was speaking of a Portuguese town on the coast which I knew was some forty miles from the frontier at the Rio Guardiana. The frontier of my country.

Sophia was already on deck with both our cases. And she was looking and sounding quite cheerful. "Thank goodness Luis! Imagine Morocco! Now we can go ashore. I do not like boats."

I told her to wait, and said if Humberto agreed, we would remain on board. She looked at me as if she thought I was mad. "Stay on the boat? No! Why? We have to remain here in Tangier where we can be safe. That is the arrangement!"

"No need to shout, Sophia." I turned away. "Just give me one minute." I walked forward to the bow where Humberto was checking the timber and speaking with Telmo. I had a few quiet words. He nodded and said it was possible for us to remain if that was what we wished. On returning to Sophia I said "Put the cases down. We stay on board." And I paused for a moment to get the message clear. Then I added "Just as far as Olhao."

She looked at me in astonishment, and could hardly get the words out. "Olhao? But that's … that's, you mean?"

I smiled. "I mean Olhao. Perhaps you have heard of it?"

She dropped the cases. "Heard? It is Olhao by Tavira? My country!"

"Your country. Humberto goes to load a cargo of salt there!"

"I cannot believe it!"

"Alright," I said teasing her. "You can remain in Tangier. I will go to Olhao with Humberto for the salt!"

She thumped me on the chest and cried "You do not dare! You are wicked, why did you not tell me?"

"Because I did not know until five minutes ago, that is why."

She flung her arms round me and very nearly knocked me across the deck into the water such was her joy. Then we simply stood there, unashamedly hugging, like a couple of kids.

We sailed the following day, encountering rough water as we departed from the Mediterranean, leaving the great rock of Gibraltar astern and setting West into the Bay of Cadiz and the cooler Atlantic. It slowed our passage, or so it seemed, because of our impatience to reach the shores of Portugal. Sophia was still in a state of disbelief and a continuing high excitement. I too felt a great sense of relief at the prospect of a safe haven, but I was worried by the realisation that we possessed no passports or papers of identity. I fancied the Portuguese authorities might not allow our entry, but I said nothing of this to Sophia.

The weather did not improve. There were rainstorms and we were forced to stay below. Sophia produced the provisions she had brought, and that evening we were pleased to be able to prepare food for Humberto and Telmo whose bed we still userped. Sophia said she could not remember Olhao, but she had once visited the village of Tavira which was close by.

Again, that night I slept very little. I kept turning over in my mind what we might do if we were not allowed entry at Olhao. Would Humberto alter his return course and deliver us after all to Tangier? I also kept thinking of our home in Granada which seemed so far away, and of Dona Vicenta and Federico and Sanchez. There was no doubt we had left them in danger, but my best hope was that Huerta de San Vicente, being the home of an important and rich family, was not likely to suffer great harm.

After two days sailing the shoreline of southern Portugal approached through the morning haze. Sophia stood on deck at the bow, staring ahead, the wind ruffling her hair. She raised her arms as if to embrace an entire continent. Her cheeks were wet with tears and I was deeply moved for her.

Part Thirteen

The River of Forgetfulness

If. a month ago, anyone had told me I would become a holiday visitor in a foreign land, I would not have believed them. The truth was I felt like a refugee in undiscovered territory.

Humberto planned to take the good ship *Esperanza* into the dock area of Olhao beyond the salt marshes and I realised we could not go ashore there. If the salt pans were in action there would be too much activity and we would be easily recognised. We had no passport or papers, and if challenged by officials we would immediately be apprehended. The only alternative open to us was to be put ashore elsewhere. It was Sophia who had an answer. She thought that there were some small uninhabited islands only a short boat ride from the main beach at Tavira. Perhaps Humberto could take us to one of them. He said he knew of them. They were called Culatra and Armona. Before entering the dock area he said he could lay up off-shore, and Telmo would take us in the ship's small lifeboat to one of the isles. We decided that was our best course. Gathering our cases again we thanked Humberto for his kind offer. I wished to pay him something for our passage and the trouble we were causing. But he waved me away.

"I think you do not know it," he rumbled, "but my boss, the young Commander Villalba, is from a millionaire family, very rich. He told me that he pays, and this he will do. Many pesetas."

We shook hands. He asked "You and your wife will return to Espana?"

I replied that I could not say, but we hoped it would be possible. It would depend on the political situation.

We waited until the hot, heavy silence of mid-day descended. Then the small boat was lowered and Telmo helped us to clamber in. He said he would put us ashore not on the island but on the beach because it appeared to be deserted. As we were entering the small channel of water dividing the islands from the mainland, Sophia was busy thinking ahead. "Remember Luis, if police or officials ask us for identity we are holiday visitors. We can be from Beja. I have been there. It is a town some kilometres inland."

I replied that it would appear strange if we were discovered carrying our cases.

"No, that is quite normal. If there are questions we are looking for accommodation! And you must keep your mouth closed. No conversation. I do the talking."

The boat grounded on the shingle and we climbed out to wade the few yards to dry land. All was quiet. The air still. Even the seabirds looked to be asleep, just drifting in the shallows. Telmo handed down our cases and said *"Jadios! Buena!"* We did not delay, waiting only long enough to thank him. Sophia was in a hurry. She ran ahead, took off her wet shoes, flung them high into the air then bent low and kissed the sand. She had returned to the land of her birth.

After stumping up to the long line of dunes we flopped down and caught our breath. The problem, said Sophia quite happily, was that we had no food. "We must find some before the night."

I was uneasy. I felt even here we were exposed. Suppose we were observed by a coastal guard or civil official? After some consideration we decided we would bury our cases in the sand against the dunes and leave some stones to mark the place. Sophia kept her shoulder bag which contained the gift of pesetas from Don Rodriguez, and my wallet for safety. Then we were ready.

We could take the short path to the village of Tavira along the side of the river. The bushes would give us some protection. I expected there must be a store, or some shops in the village. We decided to try. The mid-day heat was like a furnace. There was no wind from the sea. It was an effort, but we trudged slowly, carefully down the narrow, deserted streets. It should not have been difficult, but it was. We came upon a general store but the shutters were closed and the door was locked. We pressed the bell. No one came. It would be dangerous to wait some hours until the store opened. It was important to keep moving.

Sophia said our best course was to walk back along the beach to the marshes and towards the salt pans.

"I think Olhao is much larger than Tavira. We must take care, but we should have more luck there. We can walk up from the salt mills. But remember, Luis, if anyone approaches I must speak. You will be dumb. The Spanish people may not like the Portuguese, but in Portugal, many people, as I know, are not too much in love with Espana!"

I had no wish to speak. What was there to say? It was like a dream. Sophia had more energy than me because of her excitement, but I was now anxious and very tired. And I began to feel mean. After all, this was her land, not mine. In my homeland lives and hearts were being broken by brutality, by senseless killing and unthinking preju-dice. There were villains but there were also many innocents at risk, and suffering. I thanked God for our safety, but I did not wish to think of others who must be in so much danger. In my mind there came a vision of Sanchez. I was walking and hoping and I made a silent prayer to God that he and the Professor Aragon were still safe.

It took an hour to reach a long low building which turned out to be a fish market. A big catch was being sold and the many traders were too busy shouting and doing business deals to take notice of us. Our luck held. We walked along a promenade and made our way past a marina with some fine boats on their moorings, and turned up into the town. We did not loiter but trying to preserve an attitude of confidence we strode quickly through the Avenida da Republica and passed by a fine statue. Sophia said "Nossa Senhora de Rosario, our Lady of the Rose. I think she gives us her blessing!"

Perhaps she did. In an opening off the avenida we came upon a fishermen's Bodiga. It was small but looked surprisingly clean, with the walls painted blue and with about six tables and benches. Here at last, we were able to sit and order some food. A servant, or perhaps it was the owner of the place who appeared. He said we could eat fish. Nothing more. Mercifully, in my head I said thank you nossa Senhora. We were half way through what tasted truly like a feast, when Sophia exclaimed "Luis, look! I cannot believe it! I think that is a telephone in the corner, there on the far wall!"

✳✳✳

Three days later an open and rather battered car drew up outside the only guest house that we had found in Tavira. There was one family staying there. Two children. Sophia allowed them to understand that, like them we were having a short holiday. We could have been friendly but found it best to keep our distance and not make too much conversation.

When the car drew up I assumed it was for the family, but as I quickly learned I was wrong. Out stepped a well-dressed woman wearing a saucy beret on a blonde head of hair. It was Sophia's sister who, contacted by our telephone call, had driven all the way from Barcelos in the north. After a noisy and cheerful greeting, with much hugging and kissing Sophia introduced me.

"Here is Ginha, my sister. She is Olga Agostina Silva, but I always call her Ginha! And as I told you after the phone, Juvenal, her husband, who is my brother-in-law would not be here."

Overhearing this Ginha hung her head and looked away. "No. No he is not coming."

Sophia put her arms around her. I assumed that Ginha's husband had died, and felt sympathy for her. It was later that I learned he had "disappeared." I did not like to ask questions, but it seemed that he had become enamoured of a secretary in the Bank where he worked and subsequently made off with her. I was sorry for Ginha but she did not seem to be unduly troubled. At all events it was clear that sadness was not to be allowed to spoil the sisters' re-union.

We had regained our buried cases from the beach and were able to change our clothes. We thought that Ginha, after a long drive, would wish to rest, but she would have none of it. She had other ideas. "I have come only from Evora where I had a bed last night. Now," she declared, "I take you for your supper."

Sophia said she would not allow it, we would take her to supper. But Ginha was adamant. "No, no! You are refugees, you have little money. I will do it." She stuck her chin in the air and said firmly "Ginha has spoken!"

Sophia turned to me. "You do not know my sister, but I do! She has not changed except she has made her hair yellow! We will not have an argument, we will let her have her way."

The restaurant to which she took us was in a village between Olhao and Tavira. It was smaller, but smarter than the one that that we had found in Olhao. When we settled to the table Ginha wanted to hear about our journey and how we had succeeded in escaping from the "trouble" in Andalusia. She said in Portugal they had read reports of the insurgents and the violence, but not in great detail.

"Here in the north we already have refugees from Espana. Some have arrived from Badajoz I think, near the border, and there are others who came from Zamora to Porto where they are in hiding. They do not say very much. They know we are at peace and in some ways we are most fortunate. But I do not know for how long. I do not trust the government of Salazar. Perhaps we have the same troubles. He is a dictator, you know!" She added that it was said Salazar's Estado Novo (his New State) was supplying the Spanish insurgents with armaments imported through Lisboa.

"Here we have to be very careful. There are secret police and if they think you are socialist or a liberal they will put you in prison. In the north where I live it is safer. There are not so many policia in the Minho."

It was not always possible, but whenever I was able I was keeping notes in my journal and I wrote much of what had developed over the last weeks. Ginha had clearly decided that now she was in charge. She said there was always danger "round the corner" and we were to do as she ordered. I was amused and very touched by her care. She was most generous and said there was no difficulty. She would take us to her home in Barcelos. There was room for us to stay if we wished. We did. It was a strange feeling. We were illegal refugees, with no passports. And no where else to go.

Ginha's motor car did not look as if it would take us very far, but it had surprising power. We drove up through the great province of Alantejo. It was still high summer and almost as hot as Andalusia. I was weary. I slept much of the way and so did Sophia, but I observed some fine country, with fields of golden corn, also forests and cattle under the trees. I did not see any policia. I remember we crossed the Tagus on a very broken wooden bridge, but our cheerful driver took great care.

It was a long way to go and we were becoming exhausted, so we stopped for one night near a small town called Viseu which Ginha said was nearer to the coast with cooler air from the ocean. Close by we found a farm that had been converted to a guest house and there we stayed. The following day we continued north and soon after mid-day we arrived, with great relief and with stiff bones, at the small country town which was our destination.

※※※

Ginha's home was between Barcelos and Braga where she and Sophia had lived as children. Their house was no longer there, it had been destroyed to make room for new buildings, mainly shops with apartamento above. Sophia found new energy. It was all very exciting for her. I never saw her so happy. She was in her own country under a blue sky and with people speaking her own language. If I pulled a face she would say "Luis you cannot be miserable, this is now our home." I replied that we could not stay with Ginha very long, it was not fair to her. The house was not large but looked quite new. It stood at the end of a cobbled lane, and at the front and side there were wooden poles from which the leaves of vines were hanging.

Ginha told us that she was still working during the summer. "I have a small café by the sea shore near Viana. It is in Pria Norte above the rocks and pools where people come to swim and lie in the sun." She explained that it was a small business. She kept the café open from April to September. "Then the weather is not so warm and the mist comes in from the ocean." She hoped we would like to see her café while it was still open. "You can help me. I have only one boy. He is not always there, and very lazy."

Sophia said we would love to see the café. "Yes, Luis, we can help my sister, you can become a waiter for the tables, and put the chairs in the sun!"

In due course we visited Ginha's café on the shore. It was a wooden structure and had large windows that looked out upon the rocks and the ocean. Before the entrance there was a stretch of grass and that was where, as instructed, we set out two tables and some chairs

I was not a very enthusiastic waiter. Sophia was much better when serving the families and their children, but I was anxious to do my best if only to re-pay Ginha for her kindness in giving us accommodation. I did not feel we should remain in her house for too long and I told Sophia that we should start some enquiries to find somewhere to rent. Perhaps just a room would be better than nothing. She agreed, but it was Ginha who again found the answer. She said there was a small apartment in an arcade at the end of a line of shops near the town centre.

"It belongs to a friend of mine and he uses it for rental. I will ask him for you."

With Sophia I went to inspect the place and hoped, if it was free, it would not be too expensive. It turned out to be small, very small. There was a furnished living room, bedroom and a bathroom. A fourth room was, I supposed to be a kitchen, but it contained only cupboards and no cooking equipment.

We returned to Ginha and said we would take it if it was not to be occupied. I did not meet the owner, but Ginha went to see him and reported back that we could take the place if we wished. "We can arrange the finance later," she said. "It is not too much, and no difficulty. Here, as always in Portugal, people do not buy, always rental. I think there is no kitchen but that is not a problem, you can always have your meal with me if that is what you would like, or you can eat in the café! If you pay it will help my budget!"

A week later we moved in. Sophia agreed it would be our home for the present. We would hope to find a better apartment later.

The day came, as I guessed it would, when Sophia said she wanted show me where her mother and father had been married. Ginha agreed that she would drive us there. It was some way inland near a village in the valley of the Rio Lima called 'The River of Forgetfulness.' The route passed through several villages and was not so far from the border with my country. We arrived finally close to the river which was not very wide. The water looked shallow and bright. There were tall poplar trees on each bank and a surprisingly tall bridge with arches of grey stone. Ginha said it was a Roman bridge. In the distance I could see the red roofs of several houses. Sophia and Ginha immediately got out of the car and ran to the river bank. There they kneeled and bending low dipped their faces in the water to take a sip. I did not interfere. Then we sat on the bank and they said they knew it was here that their mother and father had been made man and wife by a church Minister. Sophia took my hand, and we were silent. After a short while she said "Now you see, Luis, why I am glad we were also married by a river."

I did see. But was our life now to be just a tale of two rivers? I did not wish to think of this. Hers was a river of sweet, bright water. Mine was a river of blood.

We passed back down the valley with the river growing wider as it flowed towards the ocean where Ginha's café stood. Back in Barcelos we bought a chicken and some presunto, also large rosy tomatoes and onions and garlic. We would have Frango na Pucara for supper. That cheered me up. It was my favourite meal that Sophia used to make. While the two sisters got busy in the kitchen I went out to find what Ginha called a "quiosque dos jornais." There I bought a magazine and a newspaper called o Publico. I assumed it was the local paper That evening after we had consumed the delicious frango I turned a page of the newspaper I wish I had never seen. Under the foreign news section the blinding headline was large and black. Ginha translated it for me. It read 'Granada falls. Spain's celebrated poet reported killed.'

Part Fourteen

Requiem

Sophia and Ginha heard my cry and they came running. They thought I had fallen or hurt myself. I had not fallen. The sky had. Disaster. I could not believe it. I did not want to believe it. Perhaps it was not true, a news report can be mistaken. Granada fallen? That was not hard to understand for I had long suspected it would happen. It was inevitable. But no. Not Federico. Had we not left him safe with Don Rodriguez and Dona Vicenta in their home? The report did not give many details. It read that there was every likelihood the poet had died of war wounds, suffering the same fate as many other Granadinos.

Sophia came to me and she too did not want to believe Federico had died. He had been so close to both of us, as if he was our own. "How can it happen?" she exclaimed. "He is the most famous son of Espana. War I can understand, but I do not believe a Government cannot protect its heroes!"

"Sophia my love, you know as well as I that we have no government, only violence and fighting. Like a fatal illness it is spreading throughout the country, no place is spared, not even Granada. There are no heroes." Again, the bitter thought ran in my mind. If we had not been helped by the Lorca family we might not be alive today. It was a terrible irony that Don Rodriguez had helped to save us but had lost his son. Could it really be true? I asked Ginha if she had a wireless set. Maybe we could listen and hear if it would be given out on the news. She replied that she did not have a wireless but she suggested she could take us to the centre of the town where there was a restaurant which had one. "Remember to be careful at all times. There is great suspicion of all strangers."

When the three of us entered we found the place was small, crowded and thick with cigarette smoke, almost like a fog. It was little more than a Bar. There was a wireless in the corner beneath a picture of Salazar. It was playing music. When it stopped there was a report but it was simply a long recital of football results. We ordered wine and Ginha asked the Barman if there had been news of the situation in Espana. He had heard only the football, but said there was a couple sitting by the far window. He had heard them talking and thought they were not Portuguese. He believed they had come from Espana two days ago.

Sophia wasted no time. Pushing her way through the crowd with glass in hand she went to them immediately. They were young. Probably husband and wife. They did not look like peasants or refugees, and wore smart clothes. Ginha and I joined Sophia and we made room so that we could talk together. It was not easy to hear because of all the noise of conversation and raised voices around us. The couple said that it was true, they had come from Salamanca and into Portugal, first to Guarda. When they learned that Sophia and I had also come from Espana and that in fact our home was in Granada, they looked very surprised. The young man stood, shook my hand. He said his name was Manuel Bernal and his wife was Rosa.

"I cannot believe you are from Granada, he exclaimed. "How could you do it? We understand it is closed, there is no way in or out. We have heard only that the Falangists have taken the Government buildings and that many have been killed in street fighting."

Not waiting to tell him of our escape I asked if he had heard news of the family of Lorca. Was it really true that Federico was dead? He shook his head. "I cannot say. We believe he was taken for questioning, that was the rumour, but here the wireless gives nothing more. It is as if Granada has been cut off from the rest of the world."

His wife looked to her left and to the right to see if anyone else was listening. Then she said quietly "You can understand, here they have the Government of Salaza. His Party has sympathy with the Right in Espana. I doubt if we will hear the truth."

Her husband added "Truth is a casualty of war. We came here when we heard that the Cortes was being driven out of Madrid to Barcelona or even Valencia. But we do not know if that is true. Here there is State censorship and we cannot be sure of anything, but we believe General Franco has many brigades supporting him. A strong army."

His wife took Sophia's hand. She said she was very sorry for us because we had lost our home. "It is the same for us, and I think there are others here from the north." She shook her head. "We say to ourselves we are lucky. Portugal must be our angel now."

※※※

We waited no more than a week and then decided we had to take a risk. From Braga we boarded a train for Porto. It was not too far. Perhaps we could find more news there. Ginha remained in Barcelos. She had to go each day to her café, but she told us that it was likely we would find more reliable information in the city where there were several National newspapers.

"Your best plan is to find the Legation office for Espana to obtain papers or passports. Then, you can feel safer and, with some luck, you will hear the truth about Granada and your poet. But be very careful. If there is trouble you must alert to me. Ginha will come and explain all for you!" Porto, she said, would be safer than going all the way to Lisboa.

We found the Legation and there, after a long wait, we were given papers including a temporary visa which carried our identity and nationality. The official also answered some of the questions we put about Granada, but he was very guarded in what he would tell us. It was not very much but this information, combined with what we learned by chance from a waiter in a café, gave us what we suppose to be the truth. Some detail we already knew. He confirmed that the

Falangists and the Catholics and others of the Right had become inflamed and infuriated because in the May election the Republicans had won every single seat in the Cortes. We knew that. From the start it had been like a match to dynamite. Now what we wanted was more up to date information of what actually took place after Granada fell and became little more than a killing field.

It was not until much later that we heard accounts of the tragedy of Granada and had to believe that the facts given were the truth. The Falangists and Fascists had, as we knew, taken to the streets and Trade Unionists, Socialists, students and other supporters equally infuriated, had attempted to repel them. That was the beginning of the terrible fighting, and as we expected, many innocents who took no side at all were killed.

The new Military Governor of the Granada garrison was General Miguel Campins. Those of the Left relied upon him because he was a known Republican, but there were rebels in the garrison who opposed him. In spite of this there was at least a little 'normality.' As we knew, Federico was in the Huerta trying to take no notice of those he called the middle class trouble-makers. He had concentrated on his new play called 'The House of Bernarda Alba' which told of a family of *campesinos* with a domineering mother who would not allow her daughters to have any communication with men they loved. There was a death. It was a tragedy.

For us it was obvious that there was a tragedy that was not in a book or a drama for the stage. It was of this day and of this time. The main disaster broke but not in a way that was to be expected. At one stroke, the troops in the garrison rose against General Campins, who was their Governor. I could only imagine his astonishment. They arrested him and compelled him to sign papers which were a declaration of war. The Republican Left demanded that arms be distributed to the populace, the ordinary citizens so they could defend themselves against the uprising. But this did not happen. No weapons were available. The garrison troops stormed all the Government buildings and took them over. They arrested the

Mayor, Manuel Fernandez-Montesinos who was Federico's broth-er-in-Law, and seized every other Republican sympathiser they could lay their hands on.

Widespread panic was reported. There were firing squads who took the law into their own hands. They did not stop to interrogate and ask questions. They preferred assassinations and executions. Street gangs became violent brutally ruling every street in the city. Below, on the Vega it was a different story for there the *campesinos* were of the Left, which meant, as we knew, that most of the area surround-ing the city was Republican territory.

Despite the killings it was not until a gang raided the Huerta, and took away the caretaker, that Federico realised he could be the next to go. It was a close call. Another mob arrived and searched the house. They said they carried a warrant for his arrest. Federico hid. The family denied that he was there. He was terrified. Don Rodriguez wanted him to get out of Granada immediately and go down to the Vega. There the Republicans and other farmers who were friendly with Don Rodriguez would protect him. But Federico, confused and in fear of his life, stubbornly refused to go. His friend, the young poet Luis Rosales whose two brothers were Falangists, said he could get Federico to safety down on the Vega. But again Federico refused, saying the journey would be too dangerous.

Manuel de Falla, who was still living in a house on the edge of Granada, said he would protect Federico. He would be safe with him there because Manuel was a devout Catholic. But this did not happen. Instead, in the end Federico decided to leave Huerta de San Vicente and seek sanctuary in the house of his friend Luis Rosales. He counted on the protection of Rosales' mother who lived there. Even though he knew she was sympathetic to her Falangist sons he felt he could hide and would be protected.

The Mayor, his brother-in-law, was not protected or safe. He was taken prisoner and later several witnesses said they had seen him dragged through the streets of his own town. He was shot and then dumped in a cemetery.

The facts that Sophia and I put together are true as far as we can tell, but we can not be absolutely sure. A story of war is never clear. It is reported that a gang called at the Rosales house led by Ramon Ruiz Alonso, who had been a Conservative MP in the Cortes, but who now styled himself as a Fascist. He said he had called to take Federico away for questioning. With him were two political ruffians who were thirsty for the blood of anyone who was regarded as a Bolshie, or Red. When they called at the house only Senora Rosales was there, her sons were away. She refused to hand Federico over to them, and contacted her son Miguel who was supporting the Falangist cause elsewhere. He arrived and after much argument he declared that if Federico was taken away it would simply be for questioning. He personally would guarantee his safety. He allowed Alonzo to take Federica away with him, and understood they would go to the Civil Government building.

When Luis Rosales returned home he was horrified to learn what had happened in his absence. The following morning Jose Rosales, who was Luis's other brother, negotiated an order for the poet's release, but when he arrived to free Federico he was told that he had been taken from the building. At first it was not clear whether in fact he had been removed or not, but in the afternoon it was reported that he had been seen marched under armed guard from the a government building with another 'suspect.' They were both pushed into a car and driven away.

✳✳✳

Those were the only facts I could write with any certainty in my journal. I thought they would be the last words, and so they were to be until later I learned that the suspect with Federico was a schoolmaster, but not from Granada. I did not know him. Both men, with two young toreros were driven some distance from Granada.

When I told Sophia she was shocked. "God in Heaven! A school-master? That could have been you, Luis!" She was right. And not only schoolmasters were taken. So were doctors, civil servants and even professors because they were known to be Socialists, Communists, or Liberals or simply Republican sympathisers.

✳✳✳

The place was between the villages of Alfacar and Viznar. Federico, the schoolmaster and the two toreros were locked up in a small house there. I knew the place. Years ago I had taken children from school for lessons there to escape the mid-summer heat in Granada. It was cooler. There were olive groves for shade. Also a pool and a fountain which sprayed high into the air and which had once been named the fountain of tears. Now it became the place of execution. As night fell the prisoners were forced out to kneel down near the fountain, their hands tied behind their backs. A priest arrived to hear their confessions. Then left. The hills reverberated with the volleys of shots from the firing squad.

Espana's finest poet, a genius aged 38, a blameless and kind man who never hurt a soul but whose brilliant poems and plays aston-ished and enchanted us and countless numbers of other people, was shot in the head and the back. Helpless, with the schoolmaster and the two young bullfighters he died in agony in a pool of blood.

It was reported later, that his body, with those of the schoolmaster and the two young toreros was tossed into a ditch. Someone arrived to cover the bodies, shovelling soil and stones on top of them. An official report issued a month later stated that the poet Lorca had died of 'war wounds.' The rest was silence.

✳✳✳

It was my custom on most of the last days of summer to visit Ginha's café by the shore. There were few customers. I was waiting to hear if there would be a job for me as caretaker at the school in Barcelos where Ginha had been a teacher. Another possibility was to take paper work in a company that built ships at Viana, a town not far away. But I had no interest in work. Sometimes Sophia came with me to the shore, knowing and sharing my sorrow. It was a knife in my heart. How could my own country, my beloved Granada, commit such a heinous, senseless crime.

I thought, and not for the first time, if only Federico had agreed to go down to the Vega, to the fields by the Genil among the *campesinos.* They surely would have protected him and saved him because they loved him. It was he who, with La Barraca, had opened their eyes to a wider world that would give them hope for a better life. I thought continually of what he called the terrible anonymity of death. And I also thought of how much more he could have achieved with another thirty years to his name.

One day towards evening when we had gone to the shore to close the cafe Sophia said "Look, Luis! Here is a small boy carrying a bird in his arms to show us!"

It was a white bird, a Garca-branca. An Egret. The boy held up the bird. Its legs and a wing were broken. Clearly it was dead and the lad was in tears. Sophia tried to comfort him and attempted to take the bird from him, but he would not let her.

It was almost nightfall when she led him to the beach by the rock pools. There they dug a hole in the sand, placed the bird in it and then covered the little grave with green carob leaves. The blazing disc of the day's sun slipped down into clouds on the horizon. Tracers of light shot skywards and the azure space high above turned to bronze then gold then red as blood. A chill wind stirred. We closed and locked the café. The first of the sea mists curled about us as, hand-in-hand with the boy, we took our way home.

Author's Note

An appreciation of the sheer genius, skill and versatility of Federico Garcia Lorca can only truly be gained by witnessing his plays and by reading his poems. He wrote more than a dozen plays and nine books of poetry as well as essays, letters, and brilliantly informed and academic lectures on poetry, imagination and the creative process. Before writing this novel I had access to a number of wonderful books which illuminate his life and times and are available for all to read. They included the following:– Spain, by Juan Lalaguna, first published in the UK in 2002 by the Windrush Press in association with Cassell & Co.

The Spanish Civil War by Hugo Thomas, first published by Eyre and Spottiswoode Ltd 1961. Revised edition published by Penguin Books in 1965.

The Battle for Spain by Antony Beevor, first published by Weidenfeld & Nicholson 2006.

Federico Garcia Lorca, Collected poems, Revised Bilingual Edition Edited by Christopher Maurer, published by Farrar, Straus & Giroux, New York.

Lorca. Plays One and Plays Two, Introduced and translated by Gwynne Edwards & first published by Methuan London Ltd, 1987 & 1990.

Federico Garcia Lorca, by Ian Gibson, first published in Great Britain by Faber & Faber Ltd., London, 1989.

Lightning Source UK Ltd.
Milton Keynes UK
21 May 2010

154533UK00001B/42/P